The Circus Performers' Bar

THE CIRCUS PERFORMERS' BAR

by David Arnason

Talonbooks   •   Vancouver   •   1984

copyright © 1984 David Arnason

published with assistance from the Canada Council

Talonbooks
201 1019 East Cordova
Vancouver
British Columbia V6A 1M8
Canada

This book was typeset by Resistance Graphics and printed in
Canada by Hignell Printing Ltd.

Some of these stories were published in slightly different form in
Arts Manitoba, Dakota Review, Prairie Fire, and *Ranam.*

First printing: November 1984

Canadian Cataloguing in Publication Data

Arnason, David, 1940-
    The circus performers' bar

    ISBN 0-88922-218-5

    I. Title.
PS8551.R63C5 1984   C813'.54   C84-090457-1
PR9199.3.A76C5

C'est belle chose veoir la clairté du (vin et escuz) Soleil.

François Rabelais

Again, for Carol

Contents

The Committee

The committee is meeting again this morning. It's a thorny question and we've been hard at it for days now. We like meetings, all of us, though of course we publicly profess to detest them. For a while there was a woman on the committee, and so we weren't permitted to smoke cigars, but she soon lost interest as women do, and now we can smoke once more. She was disturbing, smelling of perfume and bathpowder at the morning meetings, and with just the slightest hint of gin on her breath at the evening meetings. She kept calling for the question, and wanting to move on to other topics. The chairman had to inform her that so far as our particular committee was concerned, there really was only one question, and it was premature to call for a vote before all the ramifications had been thoroughly explored.

Sometimes, secretaries come in and bring us coffee, or even a choice of coffee or orange juice. Sometimes there are doughnuts. Once a young man came in with an overhead projector and showed us graphs. Usually, though, there are only the seven of us. We call each other by title, we treat each other with formal dignity, and we follow *Robert's Rules of Order* with meticulous precision. Not that

11

we are dull. Oh, no. There is plenty of room for parry and thrust, for witty oratory, the clever aside, or the passionate rebuttal. Robert has left room for all of that, and we are all deeply grateful to him.

I have been on other committees, but none so satisfying. Those committees fell into patterns. Members took stands and maintained them day after day, meeting after meeting. Each time, members sat in the same chairs and made the same arguments, so that when they finally got to a vote, the outcome was inevitable. We are different. Each meeting is born afresh. Nobody sits in the same chair he sat in last meeting. Nobody ever takes the same stand on the question for two meetings in a row. I have personally spoken eloquently on the subject for as many as two hours, then so passionately rebutted my own position that even my opposition cheered and shouted, "Hear, hear." We operate in an ever-shifting mosaic of alliances and oppositions. It is clear that one day we will suddenly find ourselves in unanimous agreement, a vote will be taken and our work will be over. Then there will be shaking of hands, self-congratulation and perhaps a glass of champagne. We look forward to and fear that day.

I think we could go on forever, but the apple sits in the centre of the table, a constant reminder of our heavy responsibility. It was solid and bright the day we were struck, its red skin flecked with yellow, the marks of teeth still clear in the white flesh. Now, the flesh is yellow, the skin wrinkled and brown. It has come to resemble one of those shrunken heads certain tribes are said to value.

Our chairman is wonderful. He is wise and judicious. His bright eyes sparkle behind his rimless glasses. His little goatee wags with humour when he jokes, but is filled with dignity when he is stern. The light glints off his balding head. He knows just how long to allow a digression to continue, when to allow a point of order, and when to deny one. When we are skittish and inclined towards too much enthusiasm, he is grave and sober. When we are dispirited and tired, he is witty and urbane. He is our leader and we are fiercely loyal to him. We whisper among ourselves that he was once a colleague of Robert himself, but none of us knows if this is true.

Once, after a particularly long meeting, the youngest member invited me to join him for a drink. He is an attractive man, with his shining black hair and his Zapata moustache. When he wears his pearl-grey leisure suit and his cowboy boots, no one can help staring at him. He is slight but elegant, and it is rumoured that women fall at his feet. I can believe that.

We drank white Campari and soda, and rehearsed the meeting we had just left, conceding a point here, allowing that some compromise might need to be made there. We talked about our youth, and discovered a remarkable similarity of experience. When he was doing one thing in the East, I was doing just such a thing in the West. When I was involved politically in the South, he was working for the same ideals in the North. Once, we had even attended the same open meeting for the same purpose, though neither of us had been aware of the other's presence.

Ah, then there were wonderful days. Each evening we would meet over Campari and soda. We would agree by the hour, growing a little tipsy and making plans that even then we recognized as grandiose and impossible. At the meetings, there would be winks and nods, notes exchanged, amendments seconded and positions supported. The others became belligerent or sulky, made to feel inadequate by the quicksilver of our wit. Finally, the chairman spoke to us after a meeting. He told us there was nothing so destructive as a separate caucus in an organization, and he appealed to us to consider the good of the committee and the urgent need to resolve the question. He might have pointed to the apple, but there was no need to.

That put an end to it. Oh, there were a few fitful meetings after that, but the spark was dead. We left our Campari and sodas half finished. We sat in long brooding silences, the stubs of our Tueros cigars burning unnoticed in the ashtrays. In the meetings, we found ourselves supporting separate amendments, rising to points of privilege when the other was speaking, even voting to table discussions in which the other had a burning interest.

It seems to me the committee is beginning to lose its will. Members arrive late for meetings, or leave early, arguing other committees with pressing concerns. Members speak of wives and golf dates, unthinkable reasons at an earlier time. There is rude insistence when our chairman denies a point of order. Mysteriously, files are misplaced, and often the minutes are late or incorrect.

And still the question is unresolved. What are we to do. It is getting late, and the world is changing. Everywhere there are revolutions and uprisings. Princes are nowhere to be found, and on the mountain, in her coffin of glass, our princess is sleeping.

The Raffle

In Canada, you get a kind of conviction that you can speak French, even if you can't. You get it from the packages, which have English on one side and French on the other. *Mouchoirs* Kleenex. Kellogg's *flocons de blé*. *Cigarettes filtres*. Mostly, you read French at breakfast, when it's okay to put the packages on the table instead of putting the food into pottery bowls and jugs. You read *orignal*, then turn over the package to find out that it's a moose.

"Why do you read the packages?" Carol asks me. She takes life seriously, and likes to read about massacres, disasters and wars, though she prefers local murders.

"It's the French," I tell her. "I like to read French." Then she takes the package from me and disguises the English side. She makes me try to translate the French and I always get it wrong, even though I studied it at the university and have a certificate from Princeton saying I am fluent.

"It's the wrong kind of French," I tell her. "Ask me something about poetry. Read a description of the Corsican countryside. Let me define *crépuscule* for you."

"No," she says. "If you can't read the cornflakes box, then you can't speak French." She draws fine distinctions, which is what drew me to her in the first place, but she has a mean streak. One of our friends is an anthropology professor. She asked him a question about Claude Levi-Strauss which he couldn't answer. She sniffed in that way some women can sniff, and he hasn't been able to write an article since. He spends all his time studying Levi-Strauss, hoping she'll ask him another question, but she never does. I've begged her to give him another chance. I even picked out questions for her, but she says he's just a big baby, and if he was a real anthropologist he wouldn't be worried.

Orage. That's a thunderstorm. And *guimauve,* I think might be pineapple, though I'm not sure. I'll have to check next time I shop for groceries. I don't like pineapple, or at least I don't like very much pineapple, which is quite a different thing. We live in a French neighbourhood, but nobody will speak French to us. There was even a *quincaillerie* just a few doors down from us until it went broke when the Co-op opened another hardware store across the street. Now the Co-op has gone broke too, and you have to drive all the way into the city to buy wood screws.

I was wrong. *Guimauves* are marshmallows. Pineapples are *ananas.* I told Carol about the story I'm writing and she explained the correct words, even though she doesn't know any French. I told her I was going to demonstrate her innate mean streak. She said that a concern for getting things right was not the sign of a mean streak. She pointed out some of her good points, her generosity, her concern for other people's feelings as long as they didn't pretend they were something they weren't, her admirable restraint in not pointing out to me that I have fallen down in my commitment to do half the housework. I tried to point out that a mean streak was very different from essential meanness, of which I had not accused her. "A mean streak," I told her, "is a kind of aberrant and occasional occurrence, which by its very difference sets off essential goodness." She called it a distinction without a difference, but I think she was quoting somebody.

It was like our discussion of arrogance the other night. She often calls men arrogant, and says she doesn't like them. She called the

16

host of a TV program arrogant last night, and I asked her what she meant. She defined the word perfectly, as good as any dictionary, but I've noticed that she only thinks that physically attractive men are arrogant. I think she finds them sexy but, since she's committed to the woman's movement, she doesn't like to admit this, even to herself. I didn't tell her that, because it might be true and I don't want it to be true, and besides, she hates to be psychoanalyzed.

Anyway, the reason I bring this all up is because I won a raffle. It was a French raffle, and apparently I have won the *deuxième prix*. There were three *prix*, and I am supposed to go over to the church and pick up my *patente*. The problem is, I don't have the slightest idea what a *patente* actually is. I've consulted my *Larousse de poche*, but it doesn't list the word. I even got into the Volkswagen and drove all the way to the public library, but none of the dictionaries includes the word *patente*. And I'm not going to ask Carol, just in case she knows.

I decided to brazen it out. I went to the church and told the priest I'd come to pick up my *patente*. "Oh yes," he said, "just go down to the basement and pick it up." The basement looked as if it had been set up for a garage sale. Tables were covered with assorted objects: toasters, irons, clothes hampers, electric mixers, you name it, it was there. Everything was new, but everything looked like the cheapest model of its kind. There was nothing labelled *patente*, but it was clear that one or the other of these bits of merchandise was my prize. I went upstairs again and was leaving the church when the priest asked me, "Aren't you going to pick up your *patente*?" "No," I told him. "My car's too full. I'll pick it up later." He looked a little bewildered, but he didn't stop me, and I rushed out before I could make a fool of myself.

It's about here I start sounding paranoid. I've never won a raffle before. In fact, I've never won anything in my life, and I'll be damned if now that I've finally won, I'm going to be cheated out of my prize by the failures of the French language. I've got a stubborn streak, or at least that's what Carol says, though I don't think standing up for your rights is a sign of stubbornness. She won't let me repair things in the house any more, because she says I get into such a foul temper that it's easier to hire someone else.

I went to France once. I couldn't understand any of the conversations that went on around me. If people were talking at the next table, they might just as well have been speaking Urdu or Hindi, but the funny thing was that when I asked for things, they had no difficulty understanding me, and I could hold long conversations with innkeepers and waiters about all sorts of things. I only seemed to be able to speak the language when they were talking directly to me.

I even learned a French joke once. It was about three kittens floating down a river on a log. The log tipped over and *un deux trois* cat sank. French people don't think that joke is funny. At first they don't understand it, and when you explain, they never laugh. They seem to take their language very seriously, and they don't like people making fun of it.

Carol likes really expensive clothes. She doesn't believe in sales, because, she says, what you really get is either cheaper merchandise that looks like the real thing or clothes with flaws in them. She claims she can pick out people wearing clothes that were bought on sale. Most of the labels in her clothes are written in French. She says it's better to have fewer good clothes than a lot of cheap ugly clothes. I pointed out once that her closet was as full as anyone else's, but she said it just proved her point. Expensive clothes last longer.

She's not going to like my *patente*, whatever it turns out to be, because if it's one of the things the priest has sitting on a table in the basement of the church, then it's going to be the cheapest *patente* you can buy, and Carol feels the same way about appliances as she does about clothes. I don't care. It's my *patente*, and I'm not giving it to Oxfam for a garage sale.

I grew up almost poor. We lived on a farm out in the country, and Mom bought most of the kids' clothes at rummage sales or ordered them out of the Eaton's catalogue. She said buying expensive things was sheer vanity. Dad said that if you were going to get something that was really important, you ought to get the very best, and although most of our farm machinery was tied together with baling wire, Dad had the most expensive Case tractor they make.

I suppose that's why I married Carol. She was the freshie queen at

18

university when I was in my final year. I passed her in the hallway and she smelled so good I fell in love with her right there. All the other girls I'd ever taken out smelled like lavender soap, and in high school, some of them even smelled like Lifebuoy. If you're going to spend your life with someone, you've got to be careful about things like that. It's a little like buying a tractor.

It's expensive though. Some of that French perfume costs over a hundred dollars an ounce. You're probably wondering why Carol would even consider marrying me given her tastes. Well, it turned out that after she was voted freshie queen, the market completely dried out. Nobody asked her for a date for six months. When I finally got up enough nerve to ask for a date she would have been grateful for Attila the Hun. Now, she says it was because I had a certain barnyard appeal. All her women friends laugh when she says that. I'm not certain I've figured out exactly what she means.

I phoned my old French professor at the university to find out what *patente* means. He's actually an Italian, and I'm not sure I completely trust him. He told me once that all French cooking was based on the cuisine of northern Italy, but I read an article that said that the cuisine of northern Italy was a corruption of French cooking. He told me there was no such word as *patente*. I told him it was written right on my ticket. Then he said it must be some local *patois*, but it wasn't real French.

We're always on a diet, me and Carol, twelve months a year. If you pay two hundred dollars for a blouse, you can't afford to grow out of it. Mom always had two complete outfits, one for when she was thin and one for when she was fat. Carol thinks fat people are morally decadent. We eat a lot of vegetables. I never liked vegetables very much, and in particular, I can't stand those white asparaguses that you eat cold. They're always covered with a thin layer of slime. Even if the slime exists only in my imagination, as Carol says, I'm still not going to eat any more of them.

I didn't think Mom was going to like Carol, but she did. Carol was so sweet and helpful when she came out to the farm that Mom couldn't talk about anything else for days. And it turned out that Mom really did like expensive things. Now she comes to the city and the two of them go shopping together. Dad grumbles, but since he sold a quarter section when it became clear that I was not going to come home and take over the farm, he's got plenty of money. He's the one who got a little upset when I got married. He told me I'd got a lot of woman there, and I might have bit off more than I could chew. I think he wanted me to marry Jim Harper's daughter, she of the Lifebuoy soap, but Linda decided when she went into nursing school that she was going to be a lesbian, and that's not the kind of thing you can tell your dad.

Patente means something or other. I should have put that in quotation marks. *Patente* means "something or other." Apparently it's a catch-all term that can mean almost anything you want it to. The fellow at the service station that gives out free glasses explained it to me when I gassed up this morning. It seems I can choose any of the things sitting on the table in the church basement. They're all bingo prizes, and whenever you win a raffle at the church, you get your choice of bingo prizes. This doesn't make things much easier. I don't actually want any of those prizes, and I certainly don't need any of them. And I'm not certain how I'm going to get it into the house without causing a row.

Carol read Nancy Friday's book, *My Mother, Myself*. Now she's afraid that she's going to turn into her mother. I said that was perfectly okay, her mother is a nice lady, but could she do it gradually? Like her mother, she does not like to be teased. She pointed out her own faults with a lot more accuracy than I would have dared, then she blamed them all on her mother. Deep down, apparently, Carol is not like that at all. That was last week. This week she's reading a book called *Don't Say Yes When You Want To Say No*. I've never noticed that she had a problem in that line, but she says people are always getting her to do things she doesn't want to, like going to showers and Tupperware parties. I've noticed, though, that she only goes to ones where you bring your own bottle of wine.

I chose *une bouilloire électrique*, an electric kettle, a very small brown one with a short cord. Carol loves it. She banished the big chrome kettle to a box in the basement where it awaits emergencies. All I did was confess the whole thing, my failures in French, my

20

humiliation at the hands of the priest, my own stubbornness. She gave me a little cuddle and said it was okay, she really liked the kettle. I personally can't stand the machine. It sits there primly on the cupboard while I eat my *flocons de blé* and ponder the French on the cornflakes box. When it boils, it does so with a nasty nasal whistle, and if you listen carefully, you can tell it is trying to sing *Frère Jacques*.

The Marriage Inspector

I was singing to myself, a happy little song about love that went "I love you, yes I do," throwing in the "doo doo doo" that the backup singers would ordinarily provide, only I didn't have any backup singers, because I was in the living room vacuuming the rug. Anyway, you know the song. We've got this arrangement, Charlotte and me, where we share the household duties. I get vacuuming, laundry and dishes. She gets most of the cooking, except for salads and pancakes, and she does the shopping and takes things to the drycleaners. The rest we share pretty well fifty-fifty. I think I do more of the car repairs and she does more of the ironing, but I guess there's areas of dispute in any marriage.

So, like I said, I was doing the vacuuming when the doorbell rang, and in came this lanky guy with a brief-case and announced he was the Marriage Inspector. At first I thought it was a joke, but he hauled out his wallet, and his papers, as they say in German, were in order. He sat down in the armchair, pulled out a little notebook and a yellow HB pencil, and waited, looking expectant. I asked if he'd like a drink, but he said, no, he thought it was a little early in the day to be drinking. I didn't know what to do, so I just kept vacuuming.

The inspector jotted down a few notes in his little notebook, then when I unplugged the vacuum, he cleared his throat loudly and said, "I take it this is one of those non-traditional marriages?"

I hadn't really thought about it that way, though of course I'd heard the phrase. "Well," I said, "It's not quite the same as Mom and Dad's relationship, if that's what you mean."

"Hmmm," he said, I swear, actually, "hmmm," just like in novels. "Wife work?"

"Yes."

"Non-traditional job?"

"She's an engineer."

"Yes, I should have guessed. And you're a nurse?"

"Teacher."

"Yes, well."

"Lots of men teach," I told him, a little defensively. "In Denmark, most of the teachers, even in elementary schools, are men."

"Yes," he said. "Denmark."

"I coach the football team," I lied.

"Good, good. Money?"

"We each have our own account, and there's a joint account for household expenses."

"Pretty difficult, I guess," he said, "to keep track of the money. How much is in your wife's account?"

"I don't know."

"No, of course not."

"It's her money. It's none of my business."

"Of course. And in your account?"

"I get paid on Wednesday."

"But there's nothing in it right now?"

"No, but I don't need any."

"You're smoking." He was right. I was smoking, and I'd have to borrow money from Charlotte when she got home if I intended to continue smoking for the weekend. And she'd give me a lecture about how I should quit.

"No problem," I said. "I'll borrow a couple of bucks from Charlotte. We share easily." The last part wasn't true. Charlotte is

24

ferocious about keeping our money separate.

"Well," the Marriage Inspector said, "I have to tell you I don't approve. Marriage, as an institution, developed over countless centuries. To think that you can alter the structure yourself is sheer arrogance. There are bound to be serious problems. No, no," he said, waving away my rising objections, "I know that some traditional marriages fail, but some houses collapse and some airplanes crash. We don't encourage people to become their own architects or airplane designers because of that. This is only my personal opinion, mind you. As an inspector, I will look only at the facts. Divorce has become an expensive social problem, and we're only interested in seeing whether your particular relationship is likely to survive before we grant you a licence to have children. I'm perfectly objective."

"You don't need a licence to have children," I practically screamed at him. In fact, Charlotte and I have been trying for nearly a year to have a child. It's difficult, though, when your wife is an engineer and comes home tired a lot. She's even been keeping temperature charts, but it always seems to be the wrong time. I mean, you can hardly say to a bunch of workmen at a construction site, "I'm sorry, but we're trying to have a child, and I'm going to have to take your supervisor away for a few minutes." Workmen aren't understanding that way. How could she fire one of them after that?

"You didn't," he said smugly, "until last Thursday. The family act was changed by order-in-council, and now you do."

"That's silly," I told him, "you can't stop people from having children. If they want to have children, they'll just go ahead and have them. Then what can the government do about it? They can't just collect up all the illegal babies and murder them. They'd never win another election."

"You'll notice," he said, "that you have no children. You'll also notice that almost none of your friends have children. Why do you think that is?"

"The Pill. Birth control."

"Microwaves."

"What do you mean, microwaves?"

"Just what I said. Microwaves. Microwaves cause one hundred percent sterility. You can't have babies unless you know the antidote."

"I know lots of people who've had babies without any antidote," I told him. "The Smiths just down the street had a baby at Christmas time."

"They just got it accidentally, before there was any control on the sale of the antidote," he said smugly. "They won't have another without a licence."

"What is this antidote?" I asked.

"Asparagus."

I hate asparagus, but Charlotte loves it. She eats it about three times a week. Her first husband told me he'd divorced her purely because of the asparagus. He complained that his urine had turned green and smelled so strong that none of the people at work would have anything to do with him, and he'd been banned from the company washroom. In fact, our marriage contract contained a clause that said I never had to eat asparagus, and in turn, I was prohibited from cooking anything with coconut in it.

"We grow it in our garden," I informed him, a little smug myself this time. "Lots of people do."

"Not this year."

He was right. This year our asparagus had all turned yellow and died. Charlotte had complained about how hard it was to buy asparagus, even at the super market.

"Police sprayed it this spring. There isn't a stalk of asparagus growing anywhere except in specially guarded police compounds." He got up slowly from the armchair and picked up the book I was reading at the time and had left on the coffee table. It was the biography of Eleanor Roosevelt. He frowned, and put it back carefully, holding it in two fingers as if it were covered with some foul substance.

"It's an excellent book," I said lamely.

"Yes," he said. "Well, I must be going. Usually, the first interview is with the wife, but your wife doesn't seem to be home. I'll be back for my next visit a week from Wednesday. I'll expect to see you both then."

Wednesday is Charlotte's poker night, and I knew she wouldn't be happy about missing it. "Could you make it Thursday?" I asked. He frowned and started to make some notes in his pad. "I've got tickets to a boxing match on Wednesday," I lied.

"Ah, boxing," he sighed, brightening. "Wish I could go myself. Well then, Thursday it is." He put on his hat, a real fedora, and prepared to go. I saw him to the door, and noticed that he had a khaki-coloured trench coat draped over the front seat of his car.

"Look," he said, as he got into his car. "Make it easy on yourself. Exert a little control. You'll be happier, and it will make my job a lot easier." He shifted into reverse with a tiny grinding of gears. I noticed just the slightest squeal of tires as he pulled away.

I could see this was not going to be easy. Charlotte is not an easy person to argue with. She's a bit right wing politically, but that's to be expected, because, after all, she is an engineer, and she was going to blame this on me and my left-wing socialist cronies, even though the government doing this is as right wing as anyone could want. Don't get me wrong, though. I love Charlotte. She's stunningly beautiful, if perhaps a trifle over-libidinous. And if once or twice at an engineer's conference she's had a bit too much to drink and done a few things she regrets, well, that's life, isn't it? And besides, she's always confessed to me, and if I want to forgive her, that's nobody else's business.

Charlotte came home in a terrible temper. Apparently the subcontractor wasn't using enough steel in the cement or something, and she'd had to set him right. I mixed her a glass of Scotch and poured myself a sherry. It wasn't going to be easy to broach the subject of the Marriage Inspector.

Fortunately, I got the ideal opportunity. Charlotte often likes what she calls "a little action" before supper, especially if things have gone wrong at work. She says it helps her relieve tension. I like it to be a bit more romantic, you know, candlelight, wine, all that stuff, but there's two people in a marriage, and you've got to consider each other's needs.

We were just lying there in the bed afterwards, when I told her,

"The Marriage Inspector came by this afternoon."

"Mmmmm," she murmured. Sometimes she doesn't pay attention to what I say.

"He said we've got to have a licence to have children."

"Robin," she said, "you've got to get out of the house more. Get some of the boys together and go out for supper. You're starting to imagine things."

So I told her the whole story, down to the last detail. At first she didn't believe me. Then she went into her study and consulted a bunch of engineering texts. Microwaves make a lot more sense to her than they do to me, and when she was finished, she was in a rage. "They can't do it," she roared. "It's a communist plot, it's a violation of individual freedom." She won't wear her seatbelt either, and has twice gotten tickets for it.

The first thing she did was run out to the store to try to buy asparagus. Of course they told her they had none, but thought they might get another shipment in a month or two. I knew they weren't going to get any shipments. When the government sets out to stop something they can usually stop it. The newspapers reported that freak frosts in California had caused the asparagus shortage, but asparagus grows in more places than California. We tried phoning one of those phone-in shows, but they thought we were cranks and wouldn't even let us talk to the announcer. Apparently the government was trying to cover up things, because there were no announcements of the new policy.

When the Marriage Inspector arrived on Thursday night he was furious. He knew about our phone calls to the radio stations, and said that if we ever did that again, we'd never get a licence. Some of his colleagues down at the office had wanted to write us off right then, but he'd stood stood up for us, and they were going to give us another chance.

Charlotte was being especially tough, even though I'd warned her. She insisted on seeing his papers, but as I said, they were all authentic. She even insisted on calling our representative in Parliament, but he just said, yes, it was all on the up and up, and to co-operate and he'd see what he could do for us. He wasn't a cabinet

28

minister or anything, but he said he had some influence.

So here we are, up at Mink Lake. I'm a miner working underground. It looks good on the forms, but actually all I do is go down in the elevator then sit in a green lawn chair and push buttons to open the right door when those little railway cars full of ore come down the tracks. It's not a hard job, but you have to concentrate or else they crash into the door and spill all the ore, then somebody has to come with a shovel and fill up the little cars again. They don't like to do that, so I'm pretty careful.

Charlotte is staying home, taking care of the house. We've got a tiny little two-bedroom house out in the bush about five miles from town. It's not working out as well as it should. Charlotte is a terrible housekeeper and an even worse cook. Ever since she found out she was pregnant, she doesn't even change out of her housecoat until I get home from work. I've tried laying down the law like the Marriage Inspector told me I should, but it doesn't work as well in practice as it does in theory. If you've ever tried raising your voice to a pregnant engineer, you'll know what I mean.

Our new marriage inspector is a lot different. Actually, he only does it part time. The rest of the time he works for the telephone company. He's a young guy who dresses in cut-off jeans and a tee shirt. I guess dress codes are different out here. Charlotte says he's got great legs, but they just look like legs to me. He gave us a licence right away, and we see a lot of him, because our telephone is always breaking down. At least, Charlotte sees a lot of him, because he always comes when I'm at work, down in the mine. Sometimes I get a little jealous, but then I think a pregnant woman wouldn't be interested in anything like that. She's certainly not interested when I get home at night, and it's just as well. I get awfully tired shifting those little cars around.

I guess things are working out all right. I get drunk with the guys from shift every Friday night. Their advice is to give Charlotte a couple of good whacks to smarten her up, but I don't think I'll try that for a while. The worst thing is the asparagus. It turns out that it's me who has to eat it, and now Charlotte's talking about having six kids. I suppose it's all for the best, but there's times when I come home exhausted, and the house is in a mess, and Charlotte's sitting there in her housecoat and curlers, and I see the vacuum cleaner sitting there in the corner and I just can't help it. I straighten things up and I plug in the vacuum, and pretty soon I'm singing again.

My Baby and Me

I was sitting in my armchair drinking my third before-dinner Scotch when Patsy announced her intention to become a mother. She's my wife, Patsy, and a pretty good wife at that, better than my first two wives, who rationed the before-dinner Scotches and asked me to take out the garbage as soon as I started to read the evening paper. I told her I didn't think it was a wise idea. I told her I had already been married to two women who were mothers, and it wasn't what it was cracked up to be. I told her that babies were messy, dirty things, in-continent most of the time, cranky and bad-tempered. You can't judge just by watching them cooing in strollers. You have to live with one to know.

She wasn't convinced, even when I pointed out that we would have to postpone our holiday in Greece for twenty years, and that I would have to forget my plans to buy an Apple 2E with an eighty-character card and two disc drives. She told me she'd been to see a doctor, and the baby was on its way, everything in good working order as far as they could tell at this stage. I seemed to recollect some agreement about birth control, but she said that she'd only agreed to be responsible for the first three years, and after that it was my responsibility. It was now four years, and if I'd fallen down on the job, I had no one to blame but myself. She said if I didn't like it, I could go away and she'd live in the condominium with the baby. It would cost me thirteen hundred dollars a month and I could see the baby on alternate weekends. She'd figured it all out.

Then she went into the kitchen humming loudly. She was whipping off some pheasant *suprême* in Madeira sauce which, under the circumstances, I regarded as a suspicious and not entirely ethical act. I mixed myself a fourth before-dinner Scotch and noted with regret that there was only enough Johnny Walker Red left for two after-dinner Scotches. I could see that unless things improved, I was facing a future of measured and rationed before-dinner glasses of cheap Canadian whiskey and long evenings of nothing at all. I would not be able to afford the luxury of alcoholism in my fading years, and might have to quit entirely.

"I'm forty-nine," I shouted at the kitchen. "I'll be seventy years old on his twenty-first birthday. "Seventy-one," Patsy called back. "On her twenty-first birthday. This isn't going to happen for a few months yet. You'll be fifty."

I considered. I already had five children. They were a surly bunch and held me responsible for the failure of my first two marriages. While none of them was actually a criminal, they weren't the kind of people you'd like to get friendly with. For one thing, they had a habit of borrowing money and not paying it back. Their favourite topic of conversation was my deficiencies as a father.

"I'm a rotten father," I shouted to Patsy. "I can provide references. Just call one of my children and ask them what kind of a father I am. They'll tell you."

She wasn't convinced. "You were much too young," she told me. "A father needs maturity. You'll do much better now. Besides, you only raised boys. Boys are notoriously ungrateful. This one will be a girl. You'll like her."

When it finally did come, I went to see it in the hospital. It was tiny and red, just as I'd expected, and it seemed fiercely bad-tempered. The nurse held it up and I counted its fingers and toes like you're supposed to, and they were all there. I couldn't tell what it was, but the nurse told me it was a girl. When I visited my wife I told her that they'd given us an inadequate one, a tiny wrinkled red one, but when no one was looking I'd slipped off the name tag and exchanged it for a nice fat smooth one. She nearly believed me, and I had to stop her from running down to the nursery to make sure. You couldn't smoke in the hospital, but it didn't matter because I'd given up smoking. The hospital had a lien on the baby, and I had to pay if I wanted to get it out. When you're paying alimony and support payments to ex-wives, you've got to cut corners somewhere.

I'd sort of forgotten about babies, if you want to know the truth of it. They'd all come in a rush when I was in my twenties, and in those days they pretty much belonged to the mothers. I was busy at the time, and mostly I remember they smelled bad and made a lot of noise. I liked to dandle them during the rare moments when they were in a decent mood, and for a while I developed a real affection for a couple of them. For some reason, this seemed to make the mothers bitter. They'd sweep the babies away for dusting and powdering, and put them in beds, where they clearly didn't want to be. Then we'd have more hollering, both the mothers and the babies hollered, and I'd go out and have a few beers. I drank beer in those days.

When we got the baby home and put it in its room, which used to be my study, I thought that was it. I expected I'd look in on it again when it was about two, and if it seemed promising, I'd made an effort to get to know it when it went to school. Apparently, the rules have changed without my noticing it. When we put it in its crib, it smelled foul. Patsy said, "I'm exhausted. I think I'll lie down for a few minutes. You can change her." I told her I didn't know how, but she'd already left the room.

So I tried. I found some Pampers, which seemed a better idea than the old cloth things that babies used to wear. I got the diaper off all right, but the stink was something terrible. I ran gagging to the bathroom, and told Patsy she'd have to finish. She pretended to be asleep, so I had to try again. After a couple of more gagging runs to the bathroom, I managed to get the baby's bottom reasonably clean. Then I powdered it all up, and put the diaper on, which was easier than I had expected. After that, the baby brightened up and seemed to be trying to smile. I watched it for a while, thinking how tiny and fragile it was, and wondering how I could keep from breaking it. I think it went to sleep for a minute, then it opened its eyes and started to cry again. I picked it up carefully, keeping my hand under its head so its neck wouldn't break and making sure my thumb didn't puncture the soft spot on the top of its head. I carried it into the bedroom and shook Patsy awake with my toe. "It's hungry," I told her, "and only you can feed it." I could see we were already at war, and I am not without my resources.

For a couple of months, things went along pretty smoothly. I even got used to rye whiskey and started to like it. Patsy seemed unreasonably lazy and selfish, and I had to do a lot of the work taking care of the baby. We'd named her Melody, Melody Anne. She seemed to be an awfully smart baby, though a little devious, if you know what I mean. She'd trick you into thinking she had wet her pants, just so you'd come in and pick her up when she was supposed to be in bed. Sometimes I'd even sneak off and watch her when she was sleeping. I caught myself talking baby talk one day, and ended up drinking the entire day's supply of rye whiskey before four o'clock. Then I had a hangover in the middle of *Charlie's Angels*.

One day, a few months later, Patsy announced she was going back to work. I told her it was impossible, they wouldn't allow her to bring a baby to work, but she just bought a bunch of bottles and some milk and off she went, leaving the baby at home with me. I was working at home, writing at the kitchen table now that I didn't have a study any more, writing with a little Brother's electric typewriter since I couldn't afford an Apple 2E with a word processing program. Patsy works for an insurance company, making actuarial tables, and they have to work late a lot. I've never quite seen how you can have an emergency over actuarial tables but there you are. Anyway, that meant that me and Melody were at it nose to nose. I got really efficient, and when Patsy would come home a little late from the office, still cold from being outside and the smell of gin on her breath, she'd make Melody uncomfortable, so I'd whisk her off and powder her and put her to bed.

34

By then I'd even given up the rye whiskey, because there just didn't seem much point to it. You know, the less you drink, the worse your hangover. Besides, there's something just wrong about breathing whiskey into a little pink baby's face. So, a few months later when Patsy told me that she was leaving me and going to live with the guy who was her supervisor at work, and was taking the baby, which I could see on alternate weekends without even paying the thirteen hundred dollars, I didn't even say a word. I just packed up Melody and all the equipment you need to operate a baby, climbed on a train, and moved here. We've got a nice little flat with a view of the river. Melody's hair is long enough now that I can tie it in braids. In a few minutes, I'm going to braid her hair, put her in her stroller and we're going to go for a walk by the river, me and my baby, my baby and me.

Sons and Fathers, Fathers and Sons

There is something about fathers and sons that could do with an explanation a little less mechanical than Freud's. Anybody who is both a father and a son will know what I mean. It's a devious business, this sending your genes out into the world in a body over which you no longer have control. It calls for extreme measures, and any relationship between a father and a son is organized around extremes. Nothing is unfair.

Let me begin. I was born in a real, honest-to-goodness tar-paper shack. In that sense, my proletarian credentials are impeccable. To be perfectly honest, I was actually born in a quite up-to-date hospital, attended by a doctor who, though inclined to forgetfulness, nevertheless had all his papers. I went directly from the hospital to the shack, where I spent the next three months until my father completed the house he was building. You see, I'm trying to be honest with you, though I'm not sure that's always the best policy. That shack, however little time I spent in it, is a metaphor of my beginnings.

My son, on the other hand, was born, at least relatively, into the lap of luxury. He moved directly into a basement suite. It was a natural childbirth, not that it was intended to be. He merely came too fast for the doctor to use any of the arcane methods modern doctors prefer. He was already in this world complaining about it before they even got his mother into the delivery room. He was saved the indignity that I faced, hauled into the world by a pair of forceps, my head squeezed so out of shape that in baby pictures I look vaguely hydrocephalic.

I was by all accounts a clumsy child. I never learned how to crawl, and though I learned to walk relatively early, my first use of this newly discovered talent was to hurl myself down the basement stairs, landing fortunately on the dog, a large yellow mongrel named Bruno. Bruno, for his services in saving my infant neck, demanded his pound of flesh. He bit me in the leg, leaving me with a fear of dogs that is in no way diminished today.

My father was what in those days was called a Jack-of-All-Trades, and my clumsiness troubled him sorely. He had been a champion hockey player and a champion baseball player. It was clear to him by the time I was a year old that I was not going to be a champion anything. Later, when I went to university, I proved him wrong by becoming a champion ping-pong player, a sport which he had always loathed for its effeminacy. He congratulated me, but his congratulations came from a constricted throat and a puckered mouth.

My son, as you've probably guessed by now, is a first-rate athlete. He is the one chosen first for all teams. He plays games with a kind of easy abandon that makes difficult manoeuvres look like simple acts of nature. He has also a disquieting interest in the mechanical and the scientific, just the right qualifications for a Jack-of-All-Trades. He takes difficult things apart, things like clocks and cameras, and he puts them back together so that they continue to function. I remember my father's disgust at my own lack of coordination, the thumbs struck by hammers or caught in car doors, the machinery put hopelessly out of adjustment by my ministrations. The workings of hydraulic brakes or power steering systems remain profoundly mysterious to me, however often my father explained that only a fool could fail to see at first glance how they function.

Not that my father was really much better coordinated than I am.

He bent nails. His chisel slipped, and there was always something slightly askew in the kitchen cupboards he made. He hit fairly well-placed grounders that would never have got him to first base in a slightly better league, but were enough to make him a star in the leagues he played in. He did everything with a dogged intensity that carried his world before him. In me, he was looking for grace, but all he got was his own slight case of butterfingers without the will to overcome it.

He envies me my son who is everything he wanted me to be, everything he wanted to be himself. My son who can even sing in tune. I come from a family of tone-deaf bellowers. People often ask us what we are trying to say when we are in full song, which is even worse than being accused of being a bad singer. They can't even tell that we're trying to sing. We all own pianos and guitars and drawers full of mouth organs that none of us can play.

What is worst for my father is the knowledge that none of my son's graceful genes come from him. My son is tall and lithe, with wide shoulders and narrow hips, like the men of my wife's family, like the women of my wife's family for that. My father and his four brothers are middle-sized men with chests like barrels and short, thick, powerful legs. The women out of that mould make spectacular teenage girls, but go to fat early. My wife's family, on the other hand, call to mind greyhounds or thoroughbred horses. Thankfully, they are lazy and shiftless, as my father succinctly puts it, or else they would be unbearable.

I bear, unfortunately, a stunning resemblance to my father. At forty-five, I'm grey and balding, five-foot eight and barrel-chested. I'm a successful psychiatrist, though I look as if I should be moving mattresses, and in fact, whenever I dare to dress casually, I am mistaken for janitors and repairmen. I've tried wearing a large gold ring with diamonds in it to prevent this, but it doesn't help.

Oddly, it bothers my son that he bears no resemblance to me. He likes it when lying aunts point out some mysterious similarity in our eyes or our jawbones. There is none. All he has inherited from me is a kind of desperate insecurity and bottomless desire for praise, which I got from my father, and he, I suppose, got from his, and so on back to some frightened paleolithic cave-son stalking a mammoth, in order to satisfy the unspoken demands of his cave-father.

How do you praise a son to whom everything is easy? He is always winning something. Our house is littered with trophies, his jacket is heavy with crests. He reports all his successes, or he used to report them until he discovered they made me uncomfortable. Now he hides them, and the neighbours tell me. It is not even possible to praise his effort, because he seems to put in no effort, though of course that can't be true. I suspect that I am only able to accept as honest effort those attempts that lead you to tears of frustration.

And that, of course, brings me to our moose hunt. Don't worry, no moose will die in this story. Not a shot will be fired in anger. The entire debacle was my own fault, and though I didn't admit it then, I admit it now. The flaw was reminiscence. My father used to take me hunting when I was young, and in the cold light of day I can remember how painful those trips were: hours of huddled crouching in marshes or in frozen bushes, shivering and wet, hoping that nothing living would stray into my range so that I would have to shoot at it. Miles of walking through deep and nearly impenetrable bush carrying heavy packs full of supplies. Yet, one evening, telling my son about my youth, I seemed only to be able to remember sitting around campfires late at night, the taste of bacon and eggs and coffee cooked over an open fire, sunrise over a lake so clear it was a perfect mirror. When my son, taken in by my poetic raptures, suggested that we go hunting moose, I was as excited as he was. We sat up late making our plans.

By the next morning I had come to my senses, though not quickly enough to avoid some sort of gesture at a hunting trip. I decided to go out to Anderson Point. There had been moose there when I was young, and it had the added advantage of being thoroughly in the wilderness and yet accessible by boat, so there would be no need to carry equipment or to slug through marshes. There was an old abandoned fishing camp that would allow a roof over our heads in case of rain. I was absolutely certain of bad weather.

I tried my best to conceal the trip from my father. When he heard about it via the women, he hinted broadly that he should be invited.

I resisted, and when he was forced finally to ask if he could come, I refused, explaining that the trip was being undertaken to allow me some private moments with my son, and pointing out to my father that his seventy years would not be helpful in case of trouble. He had given up hunting himself some ten years ago, and I suggested that his retirement should not be interrupted. He in turn pointed out his greater experience, his knack at fixing outboard motors that broke down, his superior knowledge of the shoals and reefs that surrounded Anderson Point. I referred him to his recent electrocardiogram which hinted at a heart murmur, and refused to take responsibility for his demise. That left us at a standoff, and though over the next few weeks he continued to fish for an invitation, he did not press the point.

On September 22, my son Greg and I launched the eighteen-foot fibreglass boat I had rented for the occasion into the chilly waters of Washow Creek. The sixty-five-horse Mercury outboard started as smoothly as a Cadillac and the little ten-horse spare I had brought along out of my general mistrust of machinery lay comfortably in the bow. We had enough equipment and supplies to last for a month, though we only intended to be gone for three days. All my life I've been overprepared, a backup ready for any contingency.

We left at noon on a bright sunny day with a slight breeze from the north. I wound my way through the gentle curves of the creek while my son practised making moose calls with a tin can and a piece of string that he drew through the bottom. He'd read about making moose calls in some hunting magazine and, of course, his worked perfectly. It sounded much more authentic than the actual calls of moose on the tape recorder I had brought along.

When we came out of the creek into Blind Bay, the breeze had risen, and the water was getting choppy. By the time we'd crossed the four miles of the bay out into the lake itself, there were rolling swells. And by the time we reached Crow Duck Creek, whitecaps were tossing the tiny canoe that hurried out to intercept us. When we pulled my father on board, he was soaked to the skin and the canoe was half filled with water.

"I didn't decide to come until the last minute," he told us. "Good thing I didn't miss you."

"Yes," I told him, not without a little sarcasm, "that was certainly a good thing. You might have drowned or had a heart attack."

My son, on the other hand, was delighted. He pulled the canoe across the boat and strapped it on, welcoming his grandfather with unrestrained pleasure. He made the old man take off his clothes and offered him some of his own. Standing there in the boat, naked and shivering, my father looked like a figure of the damned out of a Jehovah's Witnesses' handout, but a moment later, clothed in my son's jeans and a rugby shirt, he looked almost maliciously jaunty. The only item of his own apparel that he kept was his old Minerva Gophers baseball cap that he had been threatening for years to give to the town museum. The museum had been less keen on that artifact than my father was, and so it had remained in his possession.

My father proved his necessity by pointing out hidden shoals and disguised rocks. I had no way of knowing whether these were real or imaginary, but I avoided them anyway. As a result, we arrived a couple of hours later than I had expected, and it was dark when we reached Anderson Point. I, frankly, could see nothing, but my father claimed he could tell where we were by the sound of the breakers, and my son actually said he could see a low line of buildings against the uniformly black shore. I followed their directions, and the boat crunched onto gravel right at the fishing camp.

We landed, walked the boat around a small point of land to a pier my father remembered and which was miraculously still there after twenty-five years of abandonment. We emptied the boat, dragged my overload of supplies into what had once been the main bunkhouse, and spread out our sleeping bags on the floor. My father brought out a mickey of rye, which seemed to be the only supplies he had brought, and we each had a throat-scalding swallow. My father and my son were both eager to talk, my father to conjure the death of ancient moose, my son to predict the downfall of future moose. I exerted authority both ways, turned out the flashlight, and insisted on silence.

During the night, I awoke briefly to the patter of rain and the sound of waves crashing on the shore. It was a lulling sound, and I

42

was only briefly apprehensive. When I awoke to the grey light of a feeble dawn, the sleeping bags on either side of me were empty. I clambered into my chilly clothes and went outside. The whitecaps on the lake made it clear that we would be going nowhere in the boat that day. My father was huddled over a small fire, a frying pan in his hands and a coffee pot balanced on a stick.

"Breakfast in ten minutes," he called, as cheerfully and matter-of-factly as if he had a right to be there.

I muttered an okay and went in search of my son. I found him in a filletting shed, studying the graffiti on the walls as if they were Egyptian hieroglyphs.

"Look at this," he said. "June fifteenth, 1947." The wonder in his voice made that date sound inconceivably ancient. "It says J.T. loves M.P. I wonder who they could be?"

J.T. was Jimmy Tomlinson. His father had run this camp, and Jimmy, a classmate of mine, had left school a month early each year to go out here, because his mother was the cook. M.P. would have been Marlene Perkins, my son's mother and my wife. This evidence of an almost prehistoric passion stirred me strangely. Jimmy would have been nine years old at the time of this declaration. I wondered whether his love might have been reciprocated. Marlene was a grade behind us and, frankly, I had been only marginally aware of her existence until I had returned from university one summer, found her working in a drugstore and married her. I knew she had had other lovers, of whom I was retrospectively jealous, but I hadn't known my emotions could go so far back in time.

"I don't know," I told my son. "A lot of fishermen worked here. It could be almost anyone." Jimmy Tomlinson was now an alcoholic, sunk so deep in dissipation that there was little hope for recovery. Still, he was one more scaler of my castle, one more ghost to brood about in the irrational moments just before sleep. "Come on," I said, "Grandpa's got breakfast ready."

The breakfast was delicious, marred only by my father's habit of breaking the yolks of eggs when he cooked them. It was an old family feud, and I stood firmly with my mother on the issue. The yolks of eggs should not be broken. My son, who had never eaten

43

camp-fire cooking, pronounced the meal the best he had ever tasted.

Our plan had been to raid some of the small islands around Anderson point: Fox Island, Goose Island, Little Punk Island. Moose will swim for miles in the mating season, and there was a very good chance that, with little effort, we might find our quarry. My father explained that the canoe would come in handy because moose liked to feed in the mouths of the dozen small creeks just around the point. I put a damper on the plans by announcing that the weather made it impossible. We would wait until it calmed down. If the waves were smaller in the afternoon, we might try then. My son, who was eager and knew nothing of water, found me unconvincing. My father, who knew better, but who also knew that my conservatism would prevail, argued there was no danger. We stayed.

After that, conversation died. My son took a compass and announced he was going to go into the bush to find birch bark to make more moose calls. The Indians, he explained, always made moose calls out of birch bark. My father, who, since his retirement, had got out of the habit of early rising, announced he was going back to bed. I cautioned my son against the dangers of getting lost in the bush, but having squelched one set of plans, I couldn't garner enough moral force to stop another, and he disappeared into the yellowing bush.

Left alone, I went in search of further evidence of my wife's ghostly presence in the camp. I found it carved in the walls of the slumping outhouse. J.T. loves M.P. June, 1951. It argued a persistent attraction, but left Jimmy at thirteen, not yet old enough to be considered a danger. There had been four Tomlinson boys, all of whom I had considered sullen and introspective. Here on the walls, however, was astonishing evidence of their capacity for love. They had linked their initials with most of the alphabetic possibilities, making that lonely outhouse a monument to passion.

They had also been great makers of birthday cards for their mother. These were posted in the kitchen, and I was examining them for some consistent image when my son returned, interrupting my archeological speculation.

"I got lost," he said, almost proudly. "I checked the compass and it said I was going north. I checked it again about thirty seconds later and it said I was going south."

"You got turned around," I told him. "It's easy to do."

"I didn't believe the compass," he said. "I knew I couldn't have turned around in that short a time. So, since we're on a point, I figured if I went at right angles to the north-south line, I'd have to hit the lake, and I did, and I'm here."

A small thrill of horror ran down my spine. In the line of sons, unfortunately, I have no backups, no second chances. Anderson Point is quite large enough and quite wild enough for one to be lost and not be found. I determined then that my son would not leave my sight again during the trip.

By mid-afternoon, the clouds had cleared. The whitecaps had turned into large rolling swells, and the sun, though it gave no warmth, made everything look bright and clean. We decided to go over to Fox Island, a trip of about three miles. The motor started with a sweet purr, though I turned the key convinced that it could never start. We idled slowly, because I was taking no chances with the swells, which seemed a lot larger as soon as we got around the point. Fox Island loomed ahead, a gigantic rock with sheer cliffs on the face. Around the other side, I knew, there was a gentle sloping shore, but we were making for another abandoned fish camp on the face side. There, a floating dock took you to a set of stairs carved into the cliff, and near the top was a filletting shed set into a niche so that it seemed a part of the cliff face itself. I remembered the view from there as spectacular, and it seemed the kind of reminiscence I might share with my son, recollecting it in twenty years for some future grandson.

The landing was uneventful. We tied up the boat and made our way up the stairs to the filletting shed. My son and I went into the shed to look at the view, and my father continued up the stairs to the top. The view was magnificent. We could see across Anderson Point to Washow Bay on the far side and pick out four or five other small islands. I heard a strange scuffling noise, as if someone were walking on the roof, then a thump, and suddenly my father appeared before us, looking in the window from outside. He seemed to hover a second, as if he had something he wanted to say, and then he was gone with a splash into the water below. I froze with horror, but my son was out the door in a second. I followed, and the last thing I saw was the bottom of his shoes as he dived forty feet down to the lake below.

By the time I made my way down to the bottom of the cliff, my son had dragged his grandfather up onto the floating dock and was administering mouth-to-mouth resuscitation. The old man came to, choking and spluttering and cursing, as much horrified by the touch of male lips on his, I suspect, as by his near encounter with death. I was in a rage, wanting someone to blame besides myself, and knowing there was no one. I ordered them both into the boat and started the motor. It churned into life and I headed back to Anderson Point a lot faster than I knew I should. About a hundred yards from the dock, the motor coughed and stopped. I turned the key and heard a whining hum.

Details bore me, and they'd bore you too. I could describe my soaking father, hardly out of death's kingdom and already tinkering with the motor, my modest heroic son, eager to please, helping him. I'm not going to describe that, nor am I going to describe my churlish self, bad-tempered and clumsy, getting in the way, giving orders that had no possibility of being carried out. All I can tell you is that something happened in the water, some conjunction between the two that excluded me. They looked at each other like new lovers, they spoke to each other with shy politeness, they sidestepped me like you might sidestep an aggressive puppy.

And so it went for the rest of the trip. They fixed the motor. Back at camp, they prepared supper and talked eagerly of the next day's hunt. They ignored my pleas for darkness and sat up until late, polishing off the now sacramental mickey of rye whiskey. The next day, the two of them took the canoe and hunted in the creek mouths, my decision to keep my son in sight overridden by their desire. I pleaded a headache and stayed at the camp, reconstructing the history of the Tomlinson family, *père*, *mère* and *fils*. I grew to like them for their unreserved ability to carve their feelings into trees and walls. In a moment of inspiration I went back to the outhouse, obliterated Jimmy Tomlinson's initials from the heart that also

46

contained my wife, and replaced them with my own. A petty act, you say, a futile attempt to change history which can't be changed? We'll see.

By the time I'd prepared supper my heart was brimful of love for both my father and my son. I had determined that I would wrest forgiveness from them if I had to wrestle them to ground to get it. Even when darkness came and they had still not returned I was confident. Even after I had launched the boat, rounded the point and come on the empty floating canoe, I felt no despair. I willed them onto land, chose Little Grindstone Point a mile away as the spot I would find them, waving from the shore. I went directly there, swept the shore with my powerful flashlight, and picked them out standing on the rocky beach where they had to be. I leaped from the boat before it even grounded on the shore, churned my way through the splashing waves and seized them both in a bearhug. We swirled, the three of us in a little dance of joy and love.

I refused all explanations and apologies, refused to explain how I knew where they were until we had made our way back to camp and we had finished the meal I had prepared. Then I opened the bottle of Scotch I had brought and poured us each a large ceremonial drink. I began with my version of events, a carefully embroidered version in which heroism and comic humiliation played a large part. Then my father, taking his cue, added another layer to the evolving myth. My son wound our versions together and opened new possibilities. We sat around that fire until dawn, telling and retelling what had happened, until we had a single version that belonged to us all, carved in the wordless night. To my surprise, I came out at the centre, not at the margins as I had thought I would. There was no need to forgive or ask forgiveness. The story did that for us all.

Just one postscript. The trip back was uneventful, except that the motor refused to start again, and this time we had to use the backup ten-horse. As we were driving back along the old highway, a gigantic moose stepped out of the bush and stood on the road watching us, gleaming black as if it were wet. After a brief flurry of excitement as we reached for guns, we decided that the hunt had been too much of a success to ruin it now by killing a moose. And when I got home and asked my wife about Jimmy Tomlinson, she couldn't even remember who he was.

The Figure Skater

What magic there is left in the world is wholly in the possession of figure skaters. You remember the scene in *Carnal Knowledge* where Jack Nicholson is talking to Art Garfunkel and they are overlooking a skating rink where a figure skater swirls in delicate arabesques. Nicholson and Garfunkel are both playing seedy characters. It is difficult for us to forgive Nicholson for having seduced Candice Bergen when they were in college, and just as difficult for us to forgive Garfunkel for allowing himself to be cuckolded before he has even got married. We are presented with friends, but we know that a betrayal is at the core of their relationship, making it unstable. The figure skater swirls.

The figure skater, of course, is in all respects in opposition to the carnal knowledge of the title. She is engaged in her art. She whirls and pirouettes, and is quite as free from sexual attractiveness as an angel. There is no doubt that she is a pretty girl and that her body is graceful and attractive. Nicholson and Garfunkel look down on her from above. Ann-Margret is at home. She has become fat and bad-tempered, and just now either Garfunkel or Nicholson is explaining how unsatisfying his marriage really is.

The ice, of course, has a lot to do with it. The background against which we see the figure skater is cool and smooth. Her movements are clearly made without effort. There is no question of her perspiring. She herself is neither warm nor cold. These distinctions have nothing to do with figure skaters. There are both male and female figure skaters, but when we use the term we are always speaking of women. A male figure skater, however good, can never be more than a parody. The director knew that, and there is no male figure skater in the film.

In our part of the country, winters are bitterly cold. There is no shortage of ice, but it is impossible to figure skate outdoors because the freezing arctic winds sweep down from the north, chilling the bones and piling the snow in drifts. The ice heaves and cracks. Inside, in covered skating rinks, the figure skaters change, and lace on their white boots in dressing rooms still sour with the smell of the sweat and beer of last night's hockey players. The room is rank with the smell of maleness, and the warm air blowing from the grate in the floor provides no solace.

The skaters are preparing for the town's winter carnival. Every morning at six o'clock the three senior skaters practise for two hours before they go to the high school. The younger girls will meet with their parade-marshal instructress at three in the afternoon. The school allows these girls to leave early. At four, the younger boys will practise hockey. Outside, other preparations are underway. The Kinsmen met last night to put the final touches on the pancake breakfast. They have ordered the bacon, the flour and the milk. They have chosen their shifts.

Ticket sales are going well. We have three candidates. The blonde girl is supported by the high school, the dark girl is supported by the Chamber of Commerce, and the redhead is, of course, supported by the volunteer firefighters. Whoever sells the most tickets will have their candidate become queen. The dark girl is the doctor's daughter. There is a rumour that the doctor will buy however many tickets are required to guarantee her victory. Right now, the drawings of thermometers, gauged in dollars, indicate that she is running third. We all agree that this is the best way of choosing our queen.

50

The money will go to enlarging the dressing rooms. Only the bitter tears of the two losers will deny us, and those will disappear when the pillowcases are washed.

The figure skaters have no fear of loss. They know their moment will come. The lights will darken in the arena and the spotlight will pick them out at the door of the penalty box. There will be one second of hesitation before they push away from the wooden boards, and then they will be released into the freedom of their dance. Already they have begun to change in preparation for this metamorphosis. They are silent in the hallways of the school. They clutch their books in front of their breasts with both arms. They do not speak to their friends, scarcely recognize them on the street. At home, it is no use to talk to them. They have entered the dream. Already, they are starting to glow, like sacrificial victims before some great event, and we treat them delicately, like something fragile that might break.

Art Garfunkel and Jack Nicholson, trapped in their betrayals, their disappointments and their lust, do not even see the figure skaters. At home, Ann-Margret weeps and fights with the flesh that threatens to overwhelm her. I hurry past the snow sculptures: dinosaurs and seals balancing snow balls, snow horses pulling snow sleighs, a castle made from ice with coloured lights inside. My skates are wound around my hockey stick, the stick rests on my shoulder. I drag my canvas equipment bag over the snow. I know I am not late, but I hurry as if I were.

Most of the other players are already in the dressing room when I get there. I find an open spot on the bench and start to unpack. We make the usual lewd jokes, we elbow and jostle each other, but there is a tension that makes our uproar seem subdued. The animal of a crowd out there sobers us. We are accustomed to playing before a couple of hundred people. Tonight there will be nearly three thousand. They will be jammed so tight they cannot move, and when they shout we will feel their breath on our necks.

We are, of course, playing the ancient enemy, the Other Town. They were our fathers' rivals decades ago, and they are ours now. We will win; we always win at our carnival. They win at theirs,

51

when we are the enemy. We are inhabited by the will of that fear-some crowd. When our energy flags, the inarticulate language of its cry will enter us and give us power. We know it in our flesh.

And we do win. I am aware of the brightness of the ice, the whirl of the bodies that surround me, the jolt and crunch of the collisions. I see the black crowd that surrounds us, three thousand bodies melted into one flesh, speaking with one voice. The score is close. With moments left to play, I am afraid the coach will not put me back on the ice. We are short of defencemen, and I have already played to exhaustion. Then I am slapped on the shoulder, I tumble over the boards onto the ice, out of position. By some miracle, the puck is on my stick. I lunge toward the enemy's goal, fed by the roar of the crowd. I cannot make the decision to shoot, but will alone puts the puck into the net as I fall. Then my friends fall on top of me. They grasp me in their love. Their hands, their bodies, press against me.

In the first silence after the game, I vomit alone in the washroom, unsure whether my body is reacting to my effort or to my new-found heroism. For there is no doubt, I am now a hero. But I am the wrong hero, I was not destined for this. I should have been the silent helper, and I know that others have done more heroic things during the game. But my act came at the moment of the crowd's greatest desire, and there is only room for one hero. Later in the dressing room I am showered with sacramental beer. I dress slowly, not wanting to relinquish the moment. I have seen other heroes and I know what to do. To all congratulations and insults, I respond with quiet modesty. When I leave the rink, the crowd has gone and workmen are already installing the throne for the queen and flooding the ice for tomorrow's figure skaters.

The next day, I am up early. Heroes don't last long around here, but I am safe for the time of the carnival. Everybody knows me now. People I have only seen from a distance are my friends. They shout, "Great game," and, "Way to score." I eat the Kinsmen's pancakes, I go over to the curling rink and sample the preserves on display, talk to the farm wives selling cakes and cookies and pies. I go over to the park to watch the races. The skiers have already left, winding down the river to the lake. A half dozen dog teams yelp and fight as their owners get them ready for the dog sled race. The snowshoers walk around stamping their feet, anxious to begin. They are haloed by their breath and ice has formed on the fur of their parkas. Ordinary girls are made beautiful by the circle of white fur that surrounds their faces. I am invited to join, if not to race, at least to take part in the tug of war. I refuse. I cannot take the chance that some small loss might diminish my glory.

I wander the day in a dream. Like royalty, I grace every building I enter. The slackness of the day tightens as evening approaches. The crowning of the queen, the figure skating and the ice dance all await. Then, there is the stomping line-up at the door to the rink, the excitement and the bustle, the smell of hot dogs and hamburgers. Before we are even into the bleachers, we are in a tight crush. I can smell the alcohol on the breaths of the older men, the perfume from the women. I find a place on a bench, the third row, and squeeze in beside my friends. I am still treated with courtesy and awe, but I can feel that I am already losing myself and becoming part of the crowd.

The program begins with a comic broomball game between the volunteer firefighters and the Chamber of Commerce. The firefighters wear their firehats and long red underwear. The Chamber of Commerce is dressed as a brigade of bartenders with vests and bowler hats. A clown on skates drops the ball, and the game begins. Men, out of shape and out of breath, run in a pantomime of play. We shout out their names and professions. We insult them out of our love for their goodness, their generosity, their willingness to be there on the ice for our entertainment.

Then the game is over. A tie. It is always a tie, the scorekeeper flashing numbers on the scoreboard at his own whim, without any concern for the goals scored. After that, a master of ceremonies in top hat and tails skates out to the centre of the ice. He announces the crowning of the queen. The loudspeaker plays triumphant music. The blonde girl from the high school comes from around a cardboard screen at the end of the rink. She is beautiful in a long blue dress, and she walks on the arm of the high school principal, who is still wearing his brown suit. Then, as the trumpets blare once more, the dark-haired beauty from the Chamber of Commerce comes on the arm of the manager of the Bank of Nova Scotia. Her dress is long and white. Finally, the red-headed hairdresser who is the hope of the volunteer firefighters arrives on the arm of the postmaster, who is also a firefighter.

A little figure skater in a ballet costume skates out to the master of ceremonies and hands him an envelope. The whole building is hushed, and he would not need his microphone. Still, his voice rattles through the rafters as he announces the name. It is the dark-haired girl from the Chamber of Commerce. The other two, reduced now to princesses, embrace her. They too know the models of behaviour. They ascend the throne, queen in the middle, princesses a little lower and to the side. It is clear now that if the dark-haired girl was not prettier before, she is more beautiful now. Her crowning has given her beauty, and her father's contribution has nothing to do with it.

After the fundraising amounts have been announced, the volunteers thanked and the merchants singled out for their generosity, the figure skaters begin. First, under the full glare of the lights, a dozen tiny dancers in pink hop and skip around the ice. No one falls. It is carnival, and no one falls at carnival. Then the middle group arrives. They do more difficult tricks, they form phalanxes and arrays, they swoop and dip in imitation of their older sisters. Finally, and we have all been waiting for this, the lights go down and the solos begin. The girls are of no age, their age is unimportant, they are only beautiful and pure. They are ice made flesh and allowed to dance. We who live most of our lives on ice recognize them immediately. For Nicholson and Garfunkel, the skater is mere background. They do not see her. For us, the figure skaters are the point of focus. They hold the six thousand eyes of the crowd, and it is a wonder that the focus of so many eyes does not set them aflame.

The first dancer is dressed in red. She is birdlike, swooping, hopping, spinning off in surprising ways, seeming never to come to rest. The second dancer is in blue. She moves with a slow deliberate grace, long strides, jumps that we think must bring her to disaster until her landing transforms her into a gently spinning flower. And the white dancer. There is no hesitation. We have not even seen her

54

begin. Suddenly, she is there, skimming the ice so that she hardly seems to touch it. She leaps high in the air, weightless, and lands skating backwards, as if direction had no meaning for her. She pirouettes, she whirls, she draws our cries of delight out of our throats. Time stops completely during her performance. Then she is low on the ice, her hand holding her skate, her leg extended. She spins slowly as she rises, speeding up faster and faster until she is a blur of white, what you see when you stare at a distant star. At last, she unfolds her spiral into a sweeping bow and is gone. We roar for more, and she is back. Whenever she tries to leave, our yearning voices draw her out of the darkness into the circle of spotlight in which she dances. Finally, the master of ceremonies in his top hat and tails braves our disappointment to announce that the party will begin as soon as the orchestra can set up on the stage at the end of the rink.

For just a moment the crowd holds, but then individuals separate out onto the ice, a river of movement carries people into the waiting room and cafeteria, conversations begin, the focus is lost. All the lights come on, and, suddenly isolated, we reach out to the people closest to us, asking them if they are staying for the dance, conjuring up the day's activities. Did you take part in the snowshoe race? Did you enter the snowmobile derby? Yes, yes.

Already the band is tuning up its instruments. Mack Harvey and the Deep River Boys break into *In The Mood*. My heroism permits me to claim the queen after she has danced with the mayor and the members of the Town Council. She has put on a Hudson's Bay parka over her white gown. Her black hair curls over her shoulder. I have known her for years, since we were children. Her father delivered me, sat up all night with me when I had diphtheria, the last diphtheria case in town, my main source of fame until this carnival. We dance a polka, then join the line for the bunny hop, slipping and falling on the ice. When I hold her tight in my arms for the *Tennessee Waltz*, I can see tiny beads of sweat on her upper lip.

I have a mickey of rye whiskey in my father's half-ton truck. At intermission we sneak out the side door for a drink. It is freezing cold in the truck, but the whiskey warms us, and in a few minutes the heater begins to warm up the cab. I kiss her, and she moves tighter, pressing her body against mine. We should go back to the dance, but we know we will not. Instead, fumbling somehow through our heavy clothes, we make love. We know each other. It is a rapid coupling, and if there was any joy, I can't remember it now. After it is over, we drink some more whiskey and hold each other, shivering, but not from the cold. It is her first time, and it is also mine.

The dance is over. People pour out of the skating rink into their cars and trucks, shouting good-byes. The exhaust from their motors hangs in the air, a thick blue fog. Through it, headlights look like moons on a cloudy night. We wait until most of the cars have gone. Then I slip the half-ton into gear and begin to move slowly down the street. I flick on my headlights, and they pick out a thin wisp of a girl hurrying across the road, carrying her white costume on a coat hanger. It is the figure skater, going home.

Mary Yvette

I had a wife, still have one I suppose, though the distant woman who lives at the edges of my life bears no resemblance to the wife I once had. Not that I remember her very well. I think of a girl in a bathing suit with long dark hair, but not even the yellowing photographs in our albums justifies that memory. And I have a daughter whom I love and who loves me. Somewhere along the way, between her yellow stuffed rabbit and a night of rage that I'd sooner not remember, we decided to open our love to hurt. We have chosen to let others in. She brings to me now a succession of lovers I despise, weak and worthless men who betray and damage her, and so we are both hurt.

Her name is Mary. I chose that name myself so that she would not be hurt. It is as dull and conservative as I am, but there is not much that even the cruellest children can do with it. I have noticed, if you'll forgive me a digression, that every hurt delivered to a child is returned to the world with interest later on. The fat, the weak, the accidentally bald, the acne-stricken swallow their rage until later, when they are grown up and have power, then they deliver back every humiliation, and they are not careful of their victims.

When Mary was twelve, she renamed herself. Yvette. I was

prepared for it. Most children do. But I was not prepared for her tenacity nor for her success. One day she was Yvette, and all her friends called her Yvette. Only I, in the frailness of my fatherhood, continued to call her Mary. And even I, in less than a year, surrendered to her will. Yet sometimes, even now, in my forgetfulness, I call her Mary, and sometimes she answers.

Once, when she was only Mary and the mean and brutal lovers had not yet appeared on the horizon, she took me fishing. We walked down the beach with our poles, pieces of driftwood with string and real hooks that someone had given her. She carried the can of worms we had dug up in the garden, and later laughed at my squeamishness as she baited my hook. And the wonder of it all was that we caught fish. We dropped our six feet of string into the murky water and pulled out tiny, golden perch. For a while it was a tie, four perch each, and we teased each other about who would catch the fifth and become the world's greatest fisherman. I prayed for my defeat, and whatever gods there are who look out for fathers and daughters answered. She led me home, my tiny victor, consoling me for my loss and telling me there would be another chance for me to win, though of course there never was. There never is.

Memory is so inadequate. I think I am a graceful man. I was an athlete when I was young, and the tricks of movement came easily to me. But when I remember myself with my daughter, I remember a clumsy man, awkward, with too-large hands. A man who never knew quite when to stop and damaged all the perfect moments by wanting too much.

I wonder how my wife remembers me, if she thinks about me at all. I suppose I could go and ask her, she is in the next room, but she wouldn't understand my question, or if she did she would say something to reassure me. Give her that. She does reassure me. She sees me as a man who needs reassuring. I suspect she remembers me as a man without a face, a dark figure who was there, but is now somewhere else.

Yvette brought her first lover home when she was seventeen, a narrow, hawk-faced boy with mean eyes. I believe she really was in love, though I doubt that she has been in love since. He was older,

older even that the twenty-two years he claimed, or at least I believed that at the time. He had been out of school for years, drifting around the country, and the tissue of lies he substituted for a past could only have convinced a seventeen-year-old girl. He had been everything romantic, a cowboy, a sailor, a pilot, a judo expert, thrown out of his home by a wicked stepfather. Every story was a contradiction of the other stories, every story was itself full of contradiction. He looked out at me from eyes filled with defiance.

I forbade her to see him, knowing that this would make him more attractive but trusting, I suppose, that the stuffed yellow rabbit and the golden perch would be strong enough talismans to keep him away. I was wrong, of course, you already know that. She was gone for three days, and when she returned, I whisked her off to another country. I needn't have. She'd learned enough in those three days to know that although I was wrong, I was also right, and she couldn't forgive me for that. I don't know what happened, I never asked, but I'm sure he was cruel to her and she blamed me for conjuring up his cruelty. His eyes were the colour of fishes' eyes.

Since then there have been many more, not like the first, of course, but each in his own way specializing in one form or other of human inadequacy. Or perhaps I should say male inadequacy, for it is very much in the business of being men that they fail. Perhaps it is not even something they lack that makes them failures, but the having too much of something that in moderation might be a virtue.

There was Walter. He was a pharmaceutical salesman, starting to bald much too young and given to drinking a little too early in the day. He exuded decency and devotion, and for a while I thought he might be good for Yvette. Then, I think we both discovered at the same time that he was completely without imagination, and so of course without humour. When imagination finally did come to him, it came in the form of Amway products. He was enlisted in the Amway army, he quit his job with the pharmaceutical company, and he became a devoted acolyte. Then he started to dream of the future, a dream so dull and narrow, so mean-spirited, that it gave me a glimpse of where evil begins. For a few weeks, Yvette drove him around a series of small towns, until one day he announced that he had found someone who shared his vision and left her. To my astonishment, she wept for him.

I think at first she brought these lovers to me asking for my approval, but now she brings them as a kind of revenge. And she's right, of course, I have withheld my approval, not of her but of them. Or her too for choosing them, but that's another question. But, what has she brought me to approve? Raymond, a foul-mouthed taxi-driver, giving to nudging you with his elbow as he told dirty stories, remarkable more for their cruelty than for their wit. Jack, a clergyman so ripe for defrocking that when it happened it was an anticlimax. He chewed apples with his mouth open, making enough noise to drown all conversation, and though it is petty of me, I must tell you that when he was discovered unable to explain missing church funds, I was glad. Hal, an up-and-coming young lawyer and incipient slum landlord who left town a week before the wedding, leaving me a hefty collection of bills, including some spectacular long-distance charges. Who could he have known in Paraguay?

But let me be completely fair. I did like Dennis. He was a small, dark school teacher, who paid me elaborate court, allowing me to win at golf and making himself at home in my house without the defiance or contempt of the others. He pursued Yvette with vigour, but drifted away as it became clear that she regarded him more as a brother than as a lover. And I suppose she was right. There was in him a kind of langour, a failure of will that made him more at home with children than with adults.

And now she is pregnant, and all the lovers are gone, or at least all those flawed men are gone. I don't know who the father is, and I don't want to know. If I am to have a grandchild, I don't want to wait for the emergence of some real or imaginary trait I have projected, a brutal anger, a shiftiness in the eyes, the ghost signals of dishonesty, some trick of movement in which I suddenly see the missing father. No, I would sooner think of this as a sort of modern virgin birth, something fairly immaculate.

But I'd better tell you about the night of rage. It both trivial and important, trivial in the events that engendered it and devastating in the results. Quite simply, it was a misunderstanding, a case of mistaken identity. A police officer phoned to tell me that Yvette had been identified by a clerk at a local store. She had stolen a blouse, and when they attempted to detain her, she had fled. When Yvette came home later, I repeated those charges, adding to them some charges of my own that were equally false, but even meaner. You don't need to know them. She wept and protested but I was immoveable in my patriarchal rage. I took her straight to the police, frightened and weeping though she was. Two minutes of explanation made it clear that she could not have been the one. We left with me now the supplicant, full of apology, and she the possessor of righteous rage. Nothing since has undone that breach.

And now, instead of her lovers, she has a friend, a woman named Lou who visits every day. They go to movies, or out to the zoo, or they spend evenings at their meetings. Yvette is bright and lively and more filled with affection than any time since she was Mary, and incidentally, she is thinking of changing her name back to Mary. She and Lou speak of sharing an apartment after the baby is born. Look, I'm not a fool, I know what's going on. Mary is in love. I know the words to describe this all, but I am what I am, and I am not going to use them. Mary is happy now and she has not been happy for years. I'm not sure whether I like Lou or not. I have no standard for comparison. But I am done with disapproval.

I know with a completely irrational certainty that the child will be a girl. My solicitous friends are full of sympathy for my disastrous state, while I am almost radiant with expectation. Fate's fortunate spiral has delivered me another chance. There will be plenty of time now for stuffed yellow rabbits, for fishing lines and poles, for, yes, love, drawn up like golden perch out of the immaculate water, where I will walk barefooted, free from being, ever again, the flawed and failing father.

The Boys

The waitress who delivers the pitcher of beer to the table looks uncomfortable in her uniform. She is wearing a parody of a tuxedo, except that the pants have been replaced by very tight shorts and she wears black net stockings and high-heeled shoes. Her hair is swept up into a bun that settles on one side of her head. Don tries to imagine her in a simple summer dress, and concludes that she might in fact be attractive. He tells James of his fantasy, who agrees and calls the sexuality of her costume commercially agressive. Both men are academics who are uncomfortable in the role. They dress casually, and speak to their students in an easy, vernacular way. Only when they meet alone do they allow themselves the luxury of speaking like professors.

Lately, their discussions have been about structuralist theory. Both agree that the methods of investigation they have been using for the past years are inadequate, that they must, as they put it, retool. They teach English, and so they are not unaware of the sexual implications of the word. Don likes to point out that he has recently retooled in another way. He has left his wife of eighteen years, and is now going through a bitter divorce, which, when he

63

speaks of it, sends his listeners into gales of laughter. This was not his intent at first, but he has discovered that an attitude of mock resignation when speaking of his deepest concerns sounds funny to his friends. He uses this.

James is younger, and loves his wife. He grew up in Pincher Creek, Alberta, and likes to imagine that if he hadn't become an English professor, he would have become a cowboy. Don always points out that cowboys are never named James. Cowboys have names like Buck or Luke, or even Jim, but James is out of the question. James wears jeans and denim jackets and has a wide belt with a buckle in the shape of a steer's horns. He owns several string ties, but he only wears them at home when he is hosting a party. He says he doesn't want to become a parody of himself.

They like to mix forms of language, to speak of the young girls who take their courses as part of the carnal side-benefits of the job. They claim that the rest of their department is composed of superannuated hippies, fossilized Victorians and the scum from the broth of American manhood.

James loves his children too. He has two sons, both teen-age heroes who make all the teams and get elected the president of their classes at school. The boys court their mother in an elaborate sexual way, of which James approves. Though the oldest is sixteen and the younger fourteen, James is convinced that they are both sexually active. Don, who has only a shy sixteen year old daughter, does not like to talk about them.

The Marble Bar is a new meeting place. The place they have gone to for the past five years has renovated, and Don and James agree that the renovation has been for the worse. They liked its seedy comfort, its marked tables and working-class clientele. Since the renovations, the place is loud and crowded, filled with aggressive young people who shout at the waiters. The crowd that used to meet with Don and James has drifted away, so there has been little chance of encountering friends anyway, and so they have moved to this new location.

Only one other table in the bar is occupied. A burly Englishman who is familiar to Don and James, but whose name they do not know, is talking in hushed serious tones to a girl in large glasses. The name Marx is repeated, and they wonder if he teaches in the political science department. Don argues that the Englishman has a beautiful, gentle wife at home, but is desperately trying to seduce the girl in the glasses because she is ugly and he can smell her armpits. Englishmen, he says, are obsessed by cleanliness so are easy prey to any woman who refuses to shave her armpits. It is a game they like to play, giving histories to strangers. James argues that the Englishman is a taxi driver who has brought the girl to this particular bar near the University so he can pretend he is a professor. He argues that Canadians always assume that an English accent is a sign of education, because for years young Canadians went to Oxford and developed English accents. The girl, he claims, is a typist in a plastics factory.

Don asks James if Bob is going to drop by. James isn't sure. Bob has said he will try to make it, but he may have to take one of his kids to swimming lessons. Bob is a colleague, an economics professor who used to be a regular member of the Friday night club, as they called their gatherings. Lately, he has become very interested in his family. He brings his wife with him when he comes. Her name is Penny, and she is a small, nervous woman who has greyed early and looks older than Bob. Don and James agree that Bob has probably been discovered in an affair and is trying to rescue his marriage. When Penny comes for a beer, she pays no attention to the conversation. She seems less bored than actively hostile.

Just at the moment the waitress brings the second pitcher of beer, James waves toward the door. Don turns to see who is arriving, but he has been looking into the corner of the semi-dark bar, and his eyes do not adjust quickly. He sees the outline of a woman against the brilliant outside light. Her hair seems thick and long, and she is haloed by the purple his own eyes create around her. She moves toward them with an easy grace, a purse on a long shoulder strap swinging against her side. Don recognizes the style immediately. Julie Christie in *Billy Liar*.

She slides smoothly into the chair between the two men. She is wearing a black silk dress and Don is amazed at the clean elegance of her long legs as she struggles out of her coat. Her blonde hair stands out from her head, thick and loose as if she had just come out of the shower, but her makeup is perfect. She looks young but Don notices the delicate tracks at the edge of her eyes, the slight pucker of skin under her chin as she tucks her head downward to look into her purse. He guesses she is thirty-five.

There is some embarrassment in the jumble of introductions. James says her name is Linda. She was in a class he taught last semester. She apologizes for being late, assumes that James has prepared Don for her arrival. Don repeats his name several times, as if he were afraid she might forget it. He knows the ground now. James balances his love for his wife and children with a series of mock seductions. Linda speaks to Don in an amused, familiar way. James has told her about him. It is Don's duty to amuse her, to tell mock heroic stories about how life humiliates and defeats him at every turn. It is his specialty, and he even knows the Greek names of the rhetorical figures he employs.

Don thinks of this as step two in the process, and he sometimes teases James about it. Step one belongs entirely to James. It consists of intense literary conversations conducted over coffee. Step three is the disengagement process. Then it is Don's duty to stop being funny and evoke a world of family and community involvements that excludes the victim. At this point, they come to detest him, and Don wonders whether James's friendship is worth so much animosity.

Still, Don enjoys the initial encounters. He launches into a story of his defeat at the hands of a telephone repairman, as if this had been the subject of conversation before Linda's arrival. Linda's green eyes are cool and amused, and she responds with a very funny story of her mother's attempts to convince her to wear a girdle. The ring on her finger looks very expensive, and Don wonders at the husband whose absence fills the empty chair at the table. A doctor or lawyer? He decides he must warn James that this woman is more sophisticated than the younger women who are trapped in their net of language. He will tell James that she isn't fooled by his cowboy pose, but wants him anyway.

66

James enters the conversation to evoke her classmates. What was his name, the serious boy with the harelip? The intelligent one? James never speaks with sarcasm of anyone but his colleagues. This gives him a reputation for generosity that is important to him, and is one of the reasons why women are attracted to him. Don wonders idly whether he might not shift this woman's alliance to himself. He starts to talk about his book, the dusty archives he has worked in, the difficulty of putting complex ideas in order. She is sympathetic, and tells of her husband's fear of actually preparing the cases he must present in court. Her husband will research a case for weeks, and only write it at the last moment when he must actually face the deadline. The easy way she evokes her own network of alliances impresses Don.

James is confused. He does not want the conversation to move in this direction and he ambushes it with puns. The burly Englishman drops over to the table for a moment. He recalls a party from which he is recovering, a party at which Linda was also apparently a guest. He tells her that his wife will call her sometime during the next week about arrangements for the trip in February. When he leaves, Linda tells them he is a friend of her husband, a labour lawyer. The two couples will be spending a winter holiday in Cuba. He's breaking in a new secretary, she tells them. He is a notorious seducer. The Englishman's wife, Linda says, does not mind his seductions, but she is appalled by his taste. She feels it reflects badly on her, and has warned him to raise his sights or she will divorce him. She conjures a world of easy sexuality that makes both Don and James uncomfortable.

Though she is drinking beer, Don suspects that this is a concession to James's taste, and she will balance it with cottage cheese and fruit for the next few days. Linda's beauty seems to grow in the dim bar, and Don wonders whether James notices this. James is clearly aware of Don's treachery, and tries to compensate for it by telling stories about his youth in Pincher Creek. At some point, Don refers to James as Mellors and Linda gives him a broad wink. James does not notice, and goes on with a story of a hired hand who beat a horse with a pitchfork. Linda excuses herself to go to the powder room, and places her hand on James's as she rises. T.B., she explains, tiny bladder. Don is grateful for this touch of vulgarity.

When she has gone, James explains that he may be in love. He points out how wonderful she is, and Don agrees. It would be pointless to give warnings at this stage. He is not averse to seeing James hurt, but he is selfish enough to recognize that the shape of his own life is threatened too. He imagines Linda and James as a couple. She would not be happy in a group that spent weekends in Minneapolis rather than holidays in Cuba. He imagines her in a bikini at James's cottage at the beach. It would not work.

Don tells James he must leave. He is expected for supper with his parents. As he leaves, he encounters Linda in the hallway. She says goodbye, tells him how much fun it was to meet him, standing so close to him that he smells her faint perfume, and he is sick with desire. From the window of his car, he looks out at buildings and trees, at a blue sky that is filling with clouds, but there is nothing there he can read. Nothing at all.

Falling in Love with Alice

It hasn't been easy to fall in love with Alice. She is too perky, too convinced that her version of the world is the correct one. Whenever anything goes wrong, Alice believes that she has only to wait, and a little while later, things will correct themselves. There is a superfluity about Alice, something a little bit too much. I want to educate her. It seems to me that Alice needs educating. She looks wistfully into mirrors, and while I admit this is a highly erotic pose for a woman to take, it is damned annoying.

Alice's husband collects poetry. He does not read poetry, has in fact no use for poetry at all, but he collects it. Every day he gets parcels of books from rare-book stores in places like Sheboygan and Hull. The books are individually wrapped in newspapers from Hull and Sheboygan. Alice's husband puts the books of poetry in alphabetic order in glass-fronted book cases, and he reads the newspapers, gleaning fragmentary information about small communities all over North America. It is easy to see why Alice has affairs.

Truck drivers, construction workers and engineers are particularly attracted to Alice. I think it is her neatness that attracts them. Alice is small and compact and dresses conservatively in suits with simple blouses and brightly coloured scarves. She is the last living woman in the western world who still wears gloves even when it is not cold. When the engineers and truck drivers and construction workers make their propositions, she asks them many questions about their children, their parents, the houses that they live in. This is very confusing for men who are unaccustomed to holding conversations with women, and their lust quickly dissipates. Alice has told me that she would have no objection to sleeping with them if they would just answer her questions and ask her once more, politely.

My own lust for Alice is of quite a different sort. I make love to Alice in order to make her pay attention. I have forbidden her to ask questions during the actual event of our lovemaking. I myself have given up asking her questions at all, because I don't like the answers she gives. Alice has a fetish for the truth, her own truth of course, but truth nevertheless. I once asked her about a former lover and her answer left me squirming for days.

Alice needs information. She believes in things, and so I provide her with copies of *Scientific American* which prove that what appears to be a table is a whirling mass of molecules and atoms, with nuclei and protons and electrons. I talk to her of muons and charmed quarks. I explain molecular cell biology. I read to her from Michel Foucault's *Archeology of Knowledge* to prove to her that the self is a fiction. Alice has a very strong sense of herself, and that's damned annoying.

My own wife is not at all like Alice. My wife is a large woman who fancies herself a gypsy. She wears bright flowing dresses with rings and necklaces and bracelets. She wears her hair in a kerchief and gets drunk at parties and dances on the table. At home, she talks to herself, addressing herself by name. What she does mostly is scold herself, exhorting herself to be a better woman, to be more prompt, to pay the bills on time. There is no point in criticizing her. She has taken care of the matter herself.

My wife gets along very well with Alice's husband. He tells her snippets of information, the price of a seventy-five Honda Civic in Des Moines, Iowa, the names of the mayor and council in Fredericton, New Brunswick, the outcome of the referendum on the new high school in Fargo, North Dakota. She quotes him the poetry of Kahlil Gibran and he listens intently though, as I said, he does not like poetry. Then they drink Schlivovitz plum brandy and dance folk dances to the music from a collection of folk dances that we bought for Alice and her husband one Christmas.

At such moments, Alice and I slip into the bedroom and fornicate. We have to do this very quickly, because the longest dance on the recording is only eight minutes. Fortunately, it is the favourite selection of my wife and Alice's husband. There is very little chance to give Alice instruction during these hasty encounters, and the music and thumping from the dancers in the next room is distracting. When we return a moment after the music ends, they are sprawled in chairs, wheezing and laughing. Alice believes that they, too, fornicate during these moments, and certainly, they look more like people who have recently fornicated than we do. I do not believe this, however. I am certain my wife would sooner dance. Still, there is no way of knowing unless we spied on them, and that would not leave us sufficient time.

Alice will not remove her gloves during lovemaking. This is damned annoying. I acknowledge that a naked woman wearing only gloves is more erotic than one without gloves, but with Alice it is a sign of stubbornness. I accuse her of pretension, I argue that the gloves are rough on my skin, I speak for the beauty of perfect natural nakedness, but it is of no use. My own wife has taken to wearing anklets in bed, a dangerous business as you'll understand, and I cannot prevent that either.

It is important that I be in love with Alice. It provides a rationale for our affair, and puts it in a long tradition of *liaisons amoureuses*. Our encounters are not come by without the usual amount of lying, betrayal and treachery. There is a great deal of arranging to be done, elaborate plans to be made, risks to be taken. It would be unthinkable to go to such effort merely for physical pleasure. Beyond that, my wife is perfectly good in bed, and Alice reports that her husband is more than adequate, even in certain ways better than me, though less imaginative, as one would expect of a man who collects poetry.

Alice has no difficulty being in love with me, because she makes

71

no distinction between physical pleasure and love. I have given her *Eloise and Abelard, Tristram and Isolde* and *Romeo and Juliet* and instructed her to read them. She says they are boring, and has not finished any of them. This is damned annoying. It is difficult to fall in love with someone who is anti-intellectual, someone who blows her hair out of her eyes.

Alice adds a tiny little *r* at the end of the word *idea*. She says, "I've got a good idear." She does not do this with any other word, and refuses to admit to this flaw. Nobody else notices it, but I do. I correct her every time, but she goes on doing it, claiming she cannot tell the difference between her way and the correct way.

Alice, unclothed, looks like Venus in Botticelli's painting, *The Birth of Venus*, if, in the painting, you imagine that Venus is wearing a pair of white gloves. She adopts an attitude of modesty that borders on shame. This has nothing to do with the actual Alice, but is simply a pretension. I think she developed this particular pose by imitating the models in catalogues advertising women's undergarments. It's a highly erotic pose, but every time I speak to her about it, she blushes modestly.

Alice and I have now made love four hundred and thirteen times. She keeps track of each time in the same book that she keeps the household accounts. This is both dangerous and unromantic. At some time her husband will certainly want to examine the book, say, when he is investigated by the income tax people. Alice has divided all the possibilities of sexual union into nine classes, which she places after the decimal point. Thus the numbers read one hundred and thirty-two point six, one hundred and thirty-three point three, four hundred and thirteen point one (we were in a rush). A particularly active day may go to three decimal points, as in one hundred twelve point three six nine.

Alice loves her husband and I love my wife, that goes without saying. I like Alice's husband. We golf together. Alice likes my wife. They shop together. Alice's husband always beats me at golf, and I think that's fair, considering. Sometimes my wife golfs with Alice's husband, or at least she pulls the golf cart and collects mushrooms while he golfs. When this happens, Alice and I try for three decimal points.

Alice wrinkles her nose to express disbelief or incomprehension. When she does this, she looks like a little girl, and it's damned annoying. It's an affectation, and I've told her that, but she goes on doing it. I try to explain that if she's going to model herself on literary figures, then she should choose figures from good literature. I gave her Thomas Hardy's *Return of the Native* and suggested she model herself on Eustacia Vye, but she said Eustacia was just like my wife. She's right. It was a mistake.

Things are a bit more tricky now. My wife and Alice's husband found out about the affair, and have requested that we stop. Alice's husband packed up all his books of poetry and they moved to another house on the other side of town. My wife put away her gypsy outfit and watches me like a hawk. I haven't seen Alice for a month now, and I'm desperately afraid that some polite truck driver is going to ask her twice. I still mail her xeroxed articles from *Scientific American*, but I can't quite remember what she looks like. All I can remember are her white gloves and her mispronunciation and her wrinkled nose. Finally, I am in love with Alice.

The Drunk Woman Is Singing in My Office

The drunk woman is singing in my office. Nobody knows who she is or how she got there. There are secretaries whose job it is to keep other people out of my office, secretaries who smile and say, "No, Dr. Arnason is not in," even though I sit behind my oak door at my oak desk, twisting paper clips and throwing them into the wastebasket. They know how to tell people who telephone, "No, Dr. Arnason is with someone just now. Leave your name and number and he'll get back to you." And now, somehow, a drunk woman has got beyond all the secretaries and is in my office singing.

She is singing a mournful love song in a deep, breathy voice. There is a refrain that goes, "Come back to me my sweet," which she pronounces as "shweet," with the slurred "s" of the drinker. Her voice is not unpleasant, though there is something hard in it that I don't completely like. I have gathered the secretaries into another office to ask how the drunk woman got into my office. They inform me that no one has come past them. They suggest that she might have come in through the window, but I remind them that we are on the sixth floor, so this is unlikely. They suggest that she has been there all along, singing, but I reject this suggestion. I would surely have noticed before now.

I have sent the youngest secretary to spy on the drunk woman from behind the potted plants by the door. From there, she can see into my office. The potted plants are supplied on lease by a small firm which grows them in a nursery on the third floor of an old warehouse. Once a week the two women who own the plants come over to water them and to feed them small white tablets. The plant ladies are imperfectly beautiful, and so they have been abandoned by their husbands, who recognize the danger of imperfect beauty. The dark woman has a mole on her cheek, a small furry mouse, that is only a bit too large to be attractive. The blonde woman has high, perfect breasts, but her waist is only slightly too thick. Their husbands, who were both psychiatrists, know that such women can never be faithful and so they have cut their losses, choosing instead firm peasant girls with smaller aspirations.

The youngest secretary has come back to tell me that the drunk woman is dancing now. She is swirling around the room, dipping and rising to her own song. The youngest secretary does an imitation of the dance, balancing on the edge of falling, exaggerating all her motions. I have never noticed before that the youngest secretary is beautiful, but she has never danced for me before. I will have to see that she is transferred. I have work to do, and I cannot sit in my office thinking about the youngest secretary and her lovers, bearded lawyers who talk to her of torts, and young, blue-jeaned truck drivers who handle her roughly.

I have told the secretaries that the drunk woman in my office must be removed. I have authorized the calling of security guards, and if that fails, then the police. I have informed them that I will be gone for the day, but I have also whispered to the oldest secretary that in case of emergency I may be reached in the cocktail lounge of the Downtowner Hotel. There are never emergencies; ours is not the sort of operation that has emergencies, but it is a ritual we have evolved. The oldest secretary is very good at her job, but she needs someone she can call in case of emergency. If I did not provide this, she would leave and get a job with someone who does have emergencies. She told me once that she had wanted to be a nurse.

And now, in my dark corner of the cocktail lounge in the

Downtowner Hotel, I sip on my glass of John Jameson Irish whiskey. I prefer Old Bushmill's, but I have recently discovered it is made in the north of Ireland while John Jameson is made in the south, and in Irish matters I am a Republican. I think of the drunk woman in my office, and I am sad. Moments of truth and beauty are so rare in the world, and once more I have missed my chance. I might have gone into my office and sung with her. We might have crooned lullabies about lost love and riversides. She might have cradled me in her arms and stroked my hair. We might have cradled and sung, cradled and sung.

Or I might have gone in and danced with her. There is a radio in my office, and we could have found suitable music. We might have whirled and dipped, spinning around the room until we were both laughing and dizzy. Then we might have collapsed, still laughing, onto the couch, she might have cradled my head and stroked my hair, cradled and stroked. She might even have said she loved me.

Instead, I am alone in a bar in the middle of the afternoon, and already the security guards or the police are speaking to her in firm, stern voices. They may even be laying their hands on her to drag her out of my office. I am no fool. I know grace when I see it. I have chosen to sit in this bar drinking John Jameson with ice and water, feeling my joints and muscles relax. I have made my choices.

Square Dancers

Do square dancers, when they vote, wonder "Will this government be good for square dancing?" Do they brood on the injustice of a world that fails to take their art with sufficient seriousness? Are there grants or scholarships for young square dancers of brilliant promise? When they are together, do they tell tales of unremitting dedication that took one dancer to the top, while another dissipated his talent in drink or tragic love? Is there even a top one can get to, some final dance-off after all the local competitions, called, probably, the "North-Americans"?

In the spring, they flood the campuses of North America, the men in colourful shirts and little western string ties, the women in billowing skirts, buoyed out by massive crinolines. Where do they get those crinolines? Is there a company that specializes in producing crinolines for female square dancers? You never see those crinolines in stores, so there must be some other arrangement for selling them, mail order, perhaps, or special square-dance clothing parties, where everybody comes and tries them on. Maybe there are pro shops, like the golfers have.

They like the campuses, because the gyms are large. You can see them sitting in squares at the tables in their bright costumes. Most of them seem to be about fifty, but every so often you see a younger couple. Almost always, the male has a thin, dark moustache, and the female has a bouffant hairdo. Sometimes, there will even be a very young couple with the open faces you see in the crowd waiting to go in to a revival meeting.

Something about them reminds me of robins, though I can't quite say what. For all his red breast, the robin is a little drab, and there is something just a little drab about a gathering of square dancers, no matter how bright their clothes. The interesting thing about them is that when they change into their street clothes, you can't tell them from anybody else. You could walk past dozens of square dancers in a Woolco store, and never know it.

How do they get started? Do they discover the vocation, like a priest does, or are they enlisted by friends, who say to them after a barbecue, "Have you ever given any thought to square dancing?" Is there a missionary spirit among the committed? Do they hold membership drives? Can anyone join, or are there selection committees who ponder each candidate's rightness for admission? Is there an oath? A secret handshake?

Golfers are different. You can sometimes know golfers, even be friends with them, but unless you are a square dancer yourself, you will not know square dancers. And yet they have children, brothers, sisters. Somebody must know them. Do their families sometimes tell them, "This is madness, you can't dance your way around the continent. You're ruining your life with this obsession." Do they sometimes hire professionals to try to steal back their loved ones from the square dancers? Must they be de-programmed?

Is there a special language? Something besides do-si-do, alle-mande left and promenade? All special groups have their own argot, and so square dancers must, but why have we never heard them? We see them sitting in the university cafeterias waiting for the next competition, but when we try to eavesdrop, all we hear is a deep murmur, like water under a bridge, and the odd burst of embarrassed laughter.

Why didn't we know this was happening? Suddenly, one day they were there, thousands upon thousands of square dancers with their checked shirts, their string ties, their crinolines and their bandanas. There must have been a beginning, some period when there were only a few scattered groups. And how did it all begin? Was there some individual who decided, "It's high time there was a square dancing revival, and by gum, I'm the man to start it?" Or was it in the air, some obscure compulsion that moved individuals almost without their knowing it? Does it start as a desire to tap the foot, then perhaps a little hop on the way to the bathroom, when suddenly your arm crooks into the arm of someone with a similar compulsion, and suddenly you're dancing?

They love order, these square dancers. Their costumes match. Their squares are perfect, and they move in time to the music. When the caller cries, "Swing your corner lady," they swing, they over-and-under on command. And who is the mysterious caller, the partnerless man who orchestrates the tight patterns, what is in this for him? Is it enough just to be able to make such order with human bodies, human wills? Or is he a highly paid professional chosen for some quality of voice, some exquisite sense of timing that the rest of us can't recognize?

Only this much is known. Somewhere, outside, people are dying in El Salvador and Chile, the stockpile of bombs is rising, the lakes are dying and the sea is out of control. Inside, they bow to their partners, they take their places in the square, and when the caller's voice begins its old familiar cry, they dance, never missing a beat.

The Unmarried Sister

The Unmarried Sister is outrageous. She gets too drunk at parties and tells stories that make the men blush. She's some girl, the husbands say. The wives say it's no wonder.

The Unmarried Sister buys a red sportscar. Nobody knows how she can afford it. She drives too fast and gets two tickets the first week.

The Unmarried Sister goes to Hong Kong. She has an affair with the Chinese tour guide and nearly gets stabbed in a back alley. The wives don't believe her. The husbands say she can do better.

There is a party. Somebody brings an Unmarried Brother, tall and shy with big hands. The Unmarried Sister says, "I've got enough troubles without taking on a cripple."

The Unmarried Sister is weeping. The Brothers want to know what to do. They want to beat somebody up, but the Unmarried Sister says, "No, it isn't anything like that."

The Unmarried Sister goes to showers for younger women who are getting married. She comes with whiskey on her breath and leaves early. She brings the most expensive present and everyone is angry.

The Unmarried Sister decides to go to medical school. The Father fixes up a room for her in the basement with a separate entrance and a kitchenette, but the Unmarried Sister goes to Finland instead.

Finally, there is a man. Nobody sees him, but there are rumours he is in the white slave trade. Suddenly, the Unmarried Sister has visitors. Questions are asked. She tells them, "It's my life. I'll lead it the way I want."

The Unmarried Sister tells a joke. It is a very funny joke, but when everyone talks about it later, it seems to be a gay joke. Is the Unmarried Sister a lesbian?

The Unmarried Sister will not come for Christmas. She says she can't afford to buy presents. Everybody agrees that she shouldn't have to buy so many presents. She does come, and her presents are better than anyone else's. She doesn't know what to do with her money.

The Unmarried Sister is beautiful. Well, not beautiful, but very pretty if she'd just lose five pounds. Why will nobody marry her?

The Unmarried Sister is pissed off. Not angry or depressed, just pissed off. Why? She says it is her mother's fault. The Mother always liked the Younger Sister who is married. Why does the Mother not love the Unmarried Sister?

The Unmarried Sister makes friends with the Ex-Wives. Is this treachery?

The Unmarried Sister is hurt in a car accident. The accident is her own fault. Everybody visits her in the hospital. The nurses say she is the funniest patient they have ever had. The whole hospital loves her. After that, she doesn't get very many visitors.

The Unmarried Sister refuses to eat white bread or red meat. She disapproves of sugar. What can the Family do about this?

The Unmarried Sister dyes her hair black. This makes her look tough. Nobody knows how to tell her.

The Unmarried Sister disappears. The police are brought in. A week later, she is found in Grand Forks, North Dakota, with a married Real Estate Agent. The Unmarried Sister is furious. Is this fair to the Family who worried so much about her?

The Unmarried Sister has allergies. She cannot enter a house where there's a cat or a dog. She cannot sleep on feather pillows. She cannot eat strawberies or anything with coconut in it. She sneezes in clothing stores. When she goes to Australia, her allergies disappear. She says she might go to live in Australia, but everyone agrees this would be a mistake.

The Unmarried Sister has a dream in which all her hair falls out. She moves to another apartment.

Rapists and murderers stalk the Unmarried Sister. They hide in parking lots and peer through her windows at night. She doesn't seem to notice, but everyone agrees it would be better if she would move home and take care of the Failing Mother.

The Unmarried Sister dances. She dances the rhumba, the samba and the tango. She does foxtrots and old-time waltzes and heel-toe polkas. She can do the twist, the bunny hop, the schottische, the Charleston, the quadrille, the square dance, the cotillion, the gavotte, the minuet, the jig, the galliard, the mazurka, the butterfly, the stomp, the cakewalk, the stroll, the jive and the Highland fling. Sometimes, late at night, alone in her room, she dances, but this dance has no name.

The Economic Crisis

The president of the Kinsman Club talks to himself sometimes. Hardly worth the effort, he says, you work your fingers to the bone, setting dates for meetings, arguing with the breweries about free beer for the annual picnic, arranging for supervision of the playground, making the draw for the bonspiel and who cares? Who says, great job Joe, just hang in there Joe baby, couldn't do without you Joe? Where's the old pat on the back, the slap on the hand? Hardly worth the goddamn blue-eyed effort.

•

You think it's easy, you think you just walk out onto the stage there and take off your clothes, and that's all there is to it. You pick up your cheque and go home. It's an art you know. Hours of practise, selecting the music, doing exercises to keep yourself fit, thinking up costumes. Then they just sit there, slogging up the booze, talking about the supervisor at work. Maybe two, three people even, bother to clap. Sometimes I think it's better to be a waitress, on your feet a lot, but at least you don't have to go home and practise, and there's the odd tip. Nobody cares about art.

•

I may not even run again. What's the goddamn point. The council's loaded with assholes. You put together a package, great package, something for everybody and there's a goddamn delegation at your door complaining about property values. Sewers. There's a goddamn department to take care of sewers. Lazy bastards don't do their job, and there's a phone call at midnight. You're the mayor, do something about it. Well, I can tell you it's the lousiest salary in town and if I didn't have the Ford dealership, I couldn't even put groceries on the table. Nobody wants to pay taxes and everybody wants the potholes fixed. It's a thankless job.

•

Nothing's easy. I don't know how the hell they talked me into standing for dean. I could have been somebody, could have published my book on phenomenological reduction and got a job in a decent university instead of this little shitass college. A thousand bloody committees, and one asshole who can't keep his mouth shut on every one. And now I've got to decide whether we keep on using those little square sheets of toilet paper or shift to regular rolls like you use at home. I got a Ph.D. for this?

•

Transportation is hard hit. You wouldn't believe the kind of people I get in this cab. I tell you buddy, I seen it all. Last Friday, I pick up this couple, they want to go at it right there in the back seat. Listen, I tell them, you start that business in my cab, and out you go right here. Turns out they didn't even know each other's name, can you imagine. And that sign? No Smoking? Think they pay any attention to that? Twelve hours a day just to keep a roof over my head and the bloody taxi commission gives us a five-cent increase. Five cents? You can't buy a goddamn all-day sucker for five cents.

•

People are eating less meat. Look at the ends of those fingers. Gone.
Took them off with a cleaver in '63. Back at work the next day. You
try, you got to leave a little fat, or else you can't cook the bloody
meat. Too much gristle, they whine, all stringy. I say, you get what
you pay for. Go for a shoulder roast, and you're going to get gristle.
Look, this is all number-one meat, I hang it for nine days, most
guys, they hang it for four, maybe five days, but me? Nine. I got
three years till retirement, then I don't give a damn if they all turn
vegetarian.

•

The education budget has been cut. Thirty of the little monsters, all
day long, then they want you to go on garbage patrol during your
noon hour. Well, I don't really mean it about the kids, actually, I like
the kids, but there's some of them shouldn't be in school, know
what I mean. But try and get a social worker to look at them, and
then if they do, they say he needs special attention. Special attention. You try and give special attention when you're wiping thirty
snotty noses and tying shoes, and somebody's lost the scarf their
grandma gave them for Christmas. They've got more rules for
teachers than they have for the kids, and Lord help you if you get
sick and miss a day. They're too cheap to hire substitutes, and you
lost the few spares you've got. So you run the cross country team
and the drama club and you put on the Christmas concert and do
you get a word of thanks? Fat chance. And now this.

•

Look, I don't do this because I want to. You think it's easy, standing
on a corner in this climate? You got to dress right, and that costs.
And you should meet some of the creeps I get in this business. Look,
I'm a Catholic, there's some things I won't do. You can't even imagine what they ask for. It's pitiful, really. I went out to Calgary last

spring, but it was even worse than here. Nobody wants to pay. Seems to me, if you can't get it at home you should be willing to pay the going price. I got secretarial training, and as soon as they start hiring again, that's it for me.

•

Yeah, well I'm hanging on by the skin of my teeth. More people are worried about robberies, they're buying more dogs. But let me tell you, you got an untrained dog, it's worse than having nothing. People come here, I tell them right from the start, it's not the dog I train, it's the owner. People who can't handle their own kids think they can handle a dog. It makes me sick to walk down the street and see all those dogs running loose. They're not happy. An untrained animal isn't happy, that's a myth. If people had a little sense of responsibility, I'd have a lot more business.

•

People think you're a banker, you're some kind of priest or doctor. Sure, I feel sorry for them, but banking is a business. It's not my money, I can't lend to a bad risk. They don't know anything about economics. I try to tell them it's the government's deficit. There's only so much money to lend, and if the government borrows it, then there's that much less to loan to ordinary people. They're all after pie in the sky. This country's had it too good, too long. We've got to tighten our belts. There's jobs out there, and if you really want to work you can get them. Problem is, people are getting lazier. That's not the bank's fault.

•

The days are getting shorter. The weather is getting colder. People are hoarding when they should be spending. Nobody wants to do an honest day's work for an honest day's dollar. All of our money has been loaned to Brazil. The snow is getting deeper, there's nobody left to talk to. Something is terribly, terribly wrong.

90

Do Astronauts Have Sex Fantasies?

Do astronauts have sex fantasies? They must, of course, but has this been taken into account by the planners of space missions? Is any provision made for masturbation during long flights? What would be the effect of gamma rays on a fetus conceived and delivered in space? Is anybody in charge of this kind of investigation? We know these things are too important to be left to chance, but how are we to find out what's going on?

And what about the greenhouse effect? The melting of the polar ice caps will mean the flooding of New York and London, but isn't that a small price to pay for bananas in Manitoba? Who is going to work on the plantations in the Northwest Territories? How many Eskimos are there, and are they willing to pick things? What are we going to do with all those leftover Massey-Harris combines and four-wheel-drive Case tractors?

Are ballet dancers promiscuous? If not, how did all those rumours about them get started? Why do they walk in that funny way, even when they have quit dancing many years ago and now only teach a few of the neighbourhood girls while their husbands, who are lawyers, mix themselves Scotches and watch re-runs on TV? Why do they only marry lawyers? Where do they meet these lawyers? Do the lawyers send dozens of long-stemmed roses backstage after the performances, or are there restaurants frequented only by lawyers and ballet dancers?

Is the French language really in danger? Are English words, like viruses, creeping into French and corrupting whole sentences? Why are crêpes tastier than pancakes? How does one become a member of the French Academy? Is it possible that the president of the French Academy is a mole, an Englishman who started working in a lycée in Provence after the war, then slowly worked his way up to a teaching job at the Sorbonne, wrote a couple of books on structural linguistics, and was appointed to the French Academy? Does he dream in English?

Is it true that, because of the principles of natural selection, in eighty years all cats will be tabby? Should a cat be allowed one litter before she is spayed? Is there any way of keeping a spayed or neutered cat from growing fat? Do people think less of you if, instead of naming your cat something interesting like Oedipus or Charles, you simply call it White Cat?

What do well drillers do in winter when the ground is frozen? Do they hang around in rural cafes, having coffee with the electricians and plumbers? When the electricians and plumbers go off to work, do the well drillers hang around and tease the waitresses? Or do they take on odd jobs, cleaning a garage here, mending the shingles there? Do they sometimes wonder whether it is all worthwhile? Are their children proud of them?

How do Marxists in the United States stand up to all the contempt they face? Are they, like dentists, inclined to depression and suicide? When they lie in bed at night, thinking about death and fantasizing about all the opportunities to have sex they have missed, do they think with words like *proletariat* and *praxis*? Do they become suspicious that all their friends are working for the FBI? Are they sometimes grateful that the FBI sends beautiful female spies to seduce them and learn their secrets, women much more beautiful than they would ever have expected to sleep with? Do they sometimes marry these spies and get jobs teaching political science in small mid-western universities?

Is there any money to be made in lawn furniture? The aluminum lawn furniture with plastic webbing always breaks, and the wooden lawn furniture is always uncomfortable, so you'd think there would be room for someone to create a whole new kind of lawn furniture, wouldn't you? Is any research lab working on this question? Are there secret patents, like the patents for gas-saving carburetors which the oil companies buy up and destroy? Are these patents held by the aluminum, plastic and wood industries, while they go on turning out breakable and uncomfortable lawn furniture?

Why are piano tuners so often blind? Why do strong young men, possibly their sons, take them by the arms and lead them to pianos? Are blindness and an ear for music somehow intertwined? And what of those muscular sons, have they any plans for the future? What will they do when their frail, blind fathers die? Will they find other blind men, or will they weep with joy at their release from their fathers' musical obsessions? Will they, perhaps, holiday in Mexico for a month, then go back to school to retrain themselves as bakers or clerks?

And what of love? Must that first fierce passion decay into tolerance and mild aversion? Can love be kept alive by flowers and meals in fancy French restaurants as the newspapers tell us? Are the wealthy happier in love than we? Does regular sex help, even when neither party much cares? Do outside liaisons, amours and affairs help put the spice back in a fading relationship? Do people in the final stages of debilitating cancer still feel lust? Is anybody looking into this?

Where is Chad? Why are the Chaddians fighting one another? What is the gross national product of Chad, or is it so remote and agricultural that it does not even have a gross national product? What do they drink in Chad when they want to get drunk? Does some importer supply them with Scotch and bourbon, or do they make themselves a lusty native beer from the leaves of some native tree? What is the most popular musical group in Chad? Has any Chaddian ever written a novel of manners that chronicles a young man's rise to power?

Are the underground pipes that bring water to our houses made from asbestos? Are things being added to our water that we do not know about? Is some of our sewage seeping into the river? If things are going wrong, as we all suspect, how much money will it cost to set them right? Can we afford not to be poisoned? Does the city council know all these things but not care? Do the councillors keep bottles of pristine water from deep underground springs in their refrigerators at home?

What has become of Kohoutek's comet? Is somebody still keeping track of it, watching it dwindle into space? Do we sometimes lose discoveries because a scientist is making love to his assistant just at the moment when some life-saving but short-lived compound has precipitated in a beaker or petri jar? Who actually buys books of poetry and reads them? What happens to all the paintings of failed artists when they die? Why do you keep smoking when you know what it is doing to your lungs? Why can't you resist that extra glass of wine with supper, that extra glass of brandy after dessert, when you know what it is doing to your liver? Why are you so filled with lust and yearning and desire? Why does your weakness threaten to overwhelm everything you do? Doesn't anybody care?

The Professor

The professor, tanned like leather from his summer in the sun, his weeks in Greece in the wrong season (though it's better than nothing), meets the little long-legged girls with high, firm breasts, back from their summers on the beach. They appraise him coolly and dismiss him as a voice, though later, after Christmas break, they may look at him with a blend of pity and contempt and wonder about his sex life.

He wonders about it himself, so early in the year. As a rule, professors' wives begin as secretaries, putting their husbands through graduate school. They have a couple of kids, usually a boy and a girl, though the girl is always older. They live in condominiums and drink coffee in the mornings for the first few years after the husbands have got their first jobs. Then they discover the Women's Movement and go back to graduate school themselves. They have brief affairs with younger men, usually graduate students in English, though they themselves are always in psychology. They do much better than their husbands, and publish two important papers while still students. Their children learn to whine.

Later, though jobs are scarce, the wives manage to get positions at the same university, and they grow small moustaches. Often, though not always, they insist on separate holidays. He goes to Greece during the summer when the heat is unbearable. She goes to Mexico during Christmas with a bunch of friends, though he never knows any of their names.

Professors rarely have affairs themselves, perhaps one a lifetime, and they are always sad. It depends on the field they are in. Professors in the arts usually have affairs with middle-aged women whose husbands sell real estate or own small factories. There are brief meetings in seedy hotels and finally a long conversation in which they decide it would be impossible. Sometimes they meet later in department stores, shopping for presents for their grandchildren, but they only say hello. Professors in the humanities have affairs with impossibly young girls with glasses and straight hair, and then get in trouble with their chairmen. Science professors have affairs with the wives of their friends, and for a while everybody is uncomfortable, but it all gets straightened out in the end. Engineering and agriculture professors never have affairs, but they buy erotic magazines, and sometimes, if they are giving papers in distant cities, they go to pornographic movies. There are other faculties of course, but these follow the basic patterns, depending on how technical the field is.

The children are impossible. They are taught to read before they go to school, then the professor and his wife go to the principal and insist that their child skip a grade. The children never make the teams because they are too young and, as I said, they whine. They go to ballet school and theatre school, but they never become ballerinas or actors. They are almost always excellent swimmers. They drop out of school early, and the boys go to Europe to find themselves. The girls become secretaries, and every so often one of them marries a professor.

Professors and their wives have pets, but they are always the more exotic versions of common house pets. They keep Russian Blue cats if they are adventurous, or Siamese cats if they are not. If they choose dogs, they go for large ones, Russian wolfhounds or St. Bernards.

There are four ranks of professorship, and they are easily identifiable. Lecturers drive old Volkswagen beetles or vans. Assistant professors drive Hondas or Toyotas. Associate professors drive Volvos and full professors drive BMWs or Mercedes-Benzes, though recently Audis have become more popular. Whenever possible, the cars are diesel.

Professors live in old houses which they are restoring, and their houses always smell of fresh paint. The process begins shortly after the wives go back to school. It always turns out that the husbands have no talent for carpentry, beyond refinishing old chairs, which they do very well. The wives remove walls and install drywall. Later, their careers come first, and handymen are hired to complete the jobs. Professors worry about this sometimes, because their wives spend long hours with the working men, but nothing ever comes of this. Working men know their fantasies never come true, and are always polite.

Professors and their wives buy government bonds. Salesmen convince them of the value of saving, and they put away more than they can afford. Then they borrow money on the strength of those savings to re-paper the upstairs bedrooms. You will often see them in banks, talking intently to tellers because they think mistakes have been made in their accounts. The teller is always correct.

Professors and their wives are always left wing. Even economists who advise the government vote for left-wing candidates. Sometimes they even run for elected office, but they never win, except for school board. The long-legged girls with high, firm breasts who sit in their classes do not know this. They are the daughters of doctors and lawyers, and their professors seem indistinguishable from their parents. They do not know that their professor writes letters for Amnesty International, that he sits on the board of the John Howard Society, and he was once arrested at a civil rights sit-in.

They know nothing, those brown girls. Even though they can water ski and write poetry with some degree of promise, they are drawn to skinny boys whose pimples have still not dried up. They ride on the backs of motorcycles without wearing helmets, and without knowing why, they love horses. Many professors choose to teach eight-thirty classes in order to smell the bathpowder the girls exude early in the day.

They know nothing, those brown girls, though their lilting voices ripple through the sad, betrayed hallways. They think they will live forever. The professor in his book-lined office reads the desire in their flowing scripts. He prays for them. May they be happy. May they live long. May the loving gods release them into flowering fields, blue waters and the sun's enduring light.

The Artist

It was a splendid birth, though relatively unheralded. We weren't allowed into the delivery room, of course, but it was satisfying to wait in the waiting room with its bright draperies, its chrome and leather chairs, its large ashtrays inconspicuous in the corner. We spoke to the father for a while. He was, as you might expect, proud that the son who was about to be born would turn out to be one of the world's greatest novelists, but he insisted that the child would have a perfectly normal upbringing. He would learn to skate, play hockey, serve on the student council in school, go to picnics and later to dance.

The hospital was perfectly modern, shiny and clean with pretty nurses in starched white uniforms. It reminded me of the hospital scene in Raymond's first novel, *The Leave-Taking*. There, of course, the atmosphere is all tension, the hero wounded, the bullet lodged in his heart unremoveable. It's the scene where the beautiful but unfaithful Anya comes to visit him before the unsuccessful operation and makes her cruel joke. One wonders whether the youthful eyes will record this precise hospital and make it the setting in the great fiction.

The mother seemed distraught and in pain when she arrived. She is small, blonde, with stringy hair and pale blue eyes. There was no evidence of the sharp quality of mind described in the autobiography, or the hardness of spirit of Martha in *Late Days*. Perhaps she was not entirely the model, or it may be that she was simply distracted by her pain. At any rate, Martha's treatment of her son in the restaurant in Greece seems beyond the possibilities of this woman.

After the birth, the doctor came down to announce his success, and the father arrived with cigars. They were not very good cigars, but I suppose for an unemployed railway worker, they represented a significant gesture. The child weighed eight pounds, two ounces, and was, of course, to be named Raymond George Maddick. We were confused for a moment. The George was outside the text, but then Lewis pointed out that the George would be changed to Thomas at the christening. It was a piece of information I didn't know, and the implications were exciting. Might the chimeric hero of *Underground* be a reflection of the young Raymond's natural confusion about his lost name? You'll remember that Simon is obsessed with the name Karl, and that he meets his doppelgänger on a street in Delhi. The doppelgänger's name is, of course, Simon, just as the hero's name is, but later, during the drowning scene, they hear a distant urgent voice crying out the name Karl.

The father had to make some phone calls to other members of the family, but the doctor conducted us to the nursery to view the infant. The nurse held him up behind the glass, red-faced and squawking, looking just like any other baby. Like a father, I counted the fingers and toes. There was no sign of the mysterious birth defect that Maddick made cryptic references to in so many of his works. Perhaps the defect is meant to be seen metaphorically as a metaphysical one, something on the line of original sin. In the scene where David and Lina lie naked on the beach in *Below the Horizon*, David refers to the defect, "which no doctor dared to cure." When Lina asks him to explain, he begins by referring to "the place where the senses meet the body itself," but right at that moment they are discovered by the Count (the pun is obvious) and David undergoes the first of what he calls "his little deaths."

100

The nurse who held him up was tall and dark-haired with bright green eyes, exactly as Lina is described in *Below the Horizon*. As the infant struggled in her arms, I couldn't help wondering if her brutal murder in *Green Forces*, the second volume of the trilogy, might not have been a deep psychological response to this very moment. In fact, if I remember correctly, she is holding a cat "exactly as you would hold a child" at the moment she is struck. I spoke to the nurse after she returned the child to its bed, and she has agreed to meet with me Wednesday for coffee. She is perfectly correct that her acquaintance with Raymond Maddick has been too brief for her to offer significant biographical details, and I'll admit that my motives aren't entirely pure. I would like to know whether or not she has a mole on her thigh as does Lina. If in fact she does, this would argue prescience on Maddick's part. And, I suppose it's perfectly human to want to emulate the characters and action from your favourite works of fiction.

A little later, we were permitted to speak with the mother and child, or at least Lewis and I were. Middleton, as the youngest, had to wait in the waiting room, since only two were allowed into the mother's room at any one time. He will be allowed to visit her tomorrow. I have to admit it was a disappointment. The flood of sensation was so great that I was unable to discover anything but the most fragmentary relationships to the text. The look of surprised pain on the mother's face as the child sucked, perhaps a bit more fiercely at her breast that she had expected, called up the look on Maria's face in *Lost Labour* when she realizes the nature of Michael's message. The intent concentration of the infant reminded me, for some perverse reason, of Lina's conversation with the Count after the discovery scene. And the mother's words, "take it easy you little bugger," are the exact words that Lina addresses to her cat in the justly famous "cat scene."

I went home that night with my mind whirling with ideas. I would write the most famous biography ever written. Nothing would escape my discerning eye, no gesture, no word be too trivial for me to recount. I would establish an inter-textuality between life and art that would once and for all demolish the structuralist enterprise. I would create the ultimate text, the text that would include everything the author ever wrote, and which would capture the author himself.

The next day was Middleton's turn, and Lewis, by dint of getting to the hospital early and making promises to the impressionable young man, got himself chosen as the second visitor. It is unthinkable that two scholars with so little imagination of their own should have been chosen for so important an event. The worst is that I will have to question them intensely, and depend on their inferior observations for my research. It is infuriating.

By the time I picked up the nurse for our scheduled coffee, I had recovered somewhat from my disappointment of the day. The father and I had spoken for several hours, and he had explained his theories about national character. He doesn't seem much impressed by people from racial and ethnic groups other than his own, and seems in fact to believe that other ethnic groups constitute distinct races. Still, it is all information.

The nurse's name turned out to be Madeline, an unexpected stroke of luck. By the end of a half hour, I was calling her Lina. No one had ever called her that before, but she thought it was cute. Can you credit that she has actually been to Spain? And though she has never been the mistress of a count, she did confess to having gone what she called skinny-dipping with some of the other girls on her tour, and on a beach which, as she describes it, could be none other than the beach in *Below the Horizon*. I prevailed on her to have dinner with me the following night and, after some initial resistance, she accepted. It was only after I returned home that I realized I had entirely forgotten to discuss Maddick with her.

The following day I was late in getting to the hospital. The child was cranky, and the mother uncommunicative. Nothing seemed to connect the way it should have. I got up several times to look into the hallway, hoping for a glimpse of Lina, who had told me she would be on duty, but she did not appear. I left early, and wandered a bit out of my way toward the nursery where Lina works, until I was notified by an officious supervisor that I would have to leave.

I took Lina out to *La Vieille Gare*, one of my favourite French restaurants, where the headwaiter knows me by name. I think Lina was impressed by the cost of the dishes on the menu and by my obvious knowledge of wines. She talked of her childhood and of her experiences. She is a remarkably kind and good person, and it is easy to see why Maddick would have chosen her as the model for his finest creation. Later, we went up to my apartment for brandy and, though I will not discuss my private affairs, I can tell you that she has a small mole on her thigh, precisely as in the novel, and is a woman of even greater passion than Maddick's counterfeit.

I have told Lewis and Middleton that I am dropping out of the project. Lina and I will marry this weekend, and we intend to honeymoon in Spain. I am on sabbatical and I will devote this entire year to writing a novel. The heroine, of course, will be my lovely Lina. Maddick is, when all is considered, nothing more than a mediocre writer. His submission of Lina to the Count was reprehensible. In my work, the world will take on its proper shape.

All the Elements

This is a story that includes all the elements: a beautiful naked girl in the narrator's bed, a ruthless grab for power, a mysterious murder, a thrilling adventure, the accoutrements of wealth, virtue rewarded and vice punished, together with scenes of local colour, quaint characters, foreign places and a highly proper moral for the reader's edification. It is written in a correct style that is not without the common touch, and is quite suitable for study in the upper grades of the public schools and in colleges and universities.

I live in the village of Winnipeg Beach, a small tourist resort on Lake Winnipeg about a hundred miles north of the border between Manitoba and North Dakota. I have a winterized cottage right on the shore of the lake, from the window of which I can watch the waves crash, as they almost always do on this unusually troubled lake. I am a scholar, retired early from a series of teaching posts at some of the most prestigious universities in the world. I am too modest to name them, but among my former students I can number a considerable gathering of presidents and prime ministers, not perhaps the leaders of countries known for their wealth or for generosity towards their citizens, but names you would recognize nonetheless.

As to what I am doing living in Winnipeg Beach, or why there is a beautiful naked girl in my bed, these are more difficult questions. I can perhaps say that I have chosen this unlikely place because I am seeking peace and obscurity, and that would be largely true. The naked girl is simply a gift, and if you want further explanation you will have to wait.

I called the police about the body on the shore. I discovered it when I went for a walk this morning. The body was that of a man in his early thirties, Arab, I would guess, dressed in a three-piece pin-striped suit with black oxfords and, an unusual touch, white socks. The police were very polite. They determined that he had been shot three times in the back, and that he had no identification. I informed them that I had noticed nothing suspicious or unusual, though I suppose the naked girl in my bed might be said to be both suspicious and unusual. Still, it is impossible that she could have anything to do with the murder, and before long I shall have thought of a per-fectly reasonable explanation for her presence.

I'm back. You may not even have noticed that I was gone, but be-tween the last paragraph and this, I carried a cup of tea to the naked girl in my bed and got myself a couple of Kleenexes from the bath-room. I have either a slight cold or perhaps a touch of allergy. I don't have many allergies, but I do have a few, and they are normally trig-gered by perfume. Once, I was defeated in my lust for a beautiful newspaperwoman by my body's perverse reaction to her perfume. I broke out in welts that were so painful they made physical contact impossible.

But you don't want to hear about my humiliations. You have had plenty of humiliations of your own, some of them a good deal worse than any I might describe. But more to the point, I have a number of details I must explain, and I don't have a lot of time. I've got to go to the bank to deposit a cheque for one hundred thousand dollars. The cheque comes from the government of Libya, whose leader, I must point out, was never a student of mine. The note that accompanies it says simply, "With gratitude." This, of course, is going to make the police suspicious. In their dull-witted way, they will want to see a connection between this and the body on the beach and probably the girl, who cannot remain naked in my bed forever. (Though I suppose I could just leave her there. Still, it wouldn't be fair to you. Having brought the subject up, it would be unfair to refuse to explain it. I suppose I could regard her as a symbol, but in fact she is quite real and in no way symbolic.)

When I deposited the money in the bank (I did this when you put the book down and went into the kitchen for a glass of cold milk or to refill your drink or whatever you did while we were both gone), the teller seemed quite suspicious. In the middle of the transaction, she went off to make a phone call. To the police, no doubt. In a display of overt arrogance, I stayed and had a cup of coffee from the pot they keep in the bank for use by their customers, none of whom come there to drink coffee. I caught the manager's eye and forced him to discuss the weather with me for several minutes. When I drove off, the police car with its flashing lights was just arriving at the bank.

The naked girl was no longer naked when I returned. She was wearing a pair of my old pants and a tee shirt, doing exercises on the carpet she had arrived rolled in. She told me her name was Nadia. I asked if the pay was good for the kind of work she did. She said it depended on whether or not she made an additional commission, but this was actually her first assignment and it was too early to know whether this business was worth making into a career. Her accent sounded slightly foreign to me, but she said, no, her grandparents had come from Finland, but she had had a perfectly conventional upbringing.

We were just finishing a spot of lunch when the spy arrived. He was costumed as a fisherman in old jeans, a woollen sweater and a toque. He had an elaborate explanation for his coming to visit, including once having owned the cottage and his decision to run for the school board, but as it was perfectly obvious that he was a spy, I cut the explanation short and invited him to join us for a brandy. I introduced Nadia as my niece, my sister Hilda's girl, just down to visit for a couple of weeks.

The spy's name was Bob Larson, and he even had a stack of handouts that explained his stand on various school issues. He was, for instance, a strong proponent of physical education, and in particular of intramural non-competitive sports. I chose not to rise to the bait, but murmured sympathetically as he went through his spiel. He couldn't keep his eyes off Nadia, whose breasts were clearly visible through the thin white tee shirt. I promised to vote for him, and stood up, indicating that our interview was over. Naturally, he had to fall back on plan two, which involved looking around the old place to see what changes I had made. In another moment of perversity, a thing far too common with me, I refused to allow him to look into the bedroom on the grounds that Nadia's sister was sleeping there. Poor girl, I told him, she's exhausted. Her marriage has recently broken up and she's here to escape from her madly jealous ex-husband.

After that, all he could do was leave. Nadia had begun to sulk. She said she actually did have a sister who had recently left a madly jealous huband, and she didn't want to get her sister into any trouble. I explained that since Nadia was not her real name, there was no way the spy would be able to identify her sister. That cheered her a little, but she still seemed bored. She sat looking out the window, every so often asking me questions and suggesting we go back to the bed. I explained that I had to get this story written, and besides, I am not as young as I used to be. I suggested she take a walk on the beach and offered a baggy old jacket. She didn't seem anxious to comply until I explained that she could look for the glint of light from binoculars and identify where the watchers were sitting in the trees at the end of the cove. Then, when she came back, we could make a map. After that she was quite enthusiastic. "This is fun," she said. "It's just like a movie."

And I guess she was right. There's a way in which these things belong in movies, where you get the distance you need. That body, for instance, would have affected you more in a movie because you would have seen it directly without a narrator to point out the details. You would probably have missed the white socks, which are going to turn out to be quite important, but you'd have seen the look on the face, the sand sticking to the hair, details that aren't important to the story, but that help create an illusion of reality.

I promised some local colour, and I've given you the bank and the semi-local fisherman-spy. We're a little short on scenery, though, so I think I'll follow Nadia for a short way down the beach. It's late in the season, early October, in fact. The leaves on the trees have all turned, and along the beach, where the wind is unimpeded, most of the leaves are gone. The trees are poplar, scrub ash and maple. The shrubs are chokecherry, willow and sandcherry, though of course Nadia wouldn't have been able to identify them even if they'd had their leaves. It's not a good beach, not a swimming beach. The shore is covered with rocks, and you can see rocks sticking out of the water. The sand is actually a kind of coarse gravel that would be good for driveways, but not for spreading a blanket on. The sky is grey, piled high with clouds, and the lake is the same grey colour. Waves crash on the shore, pushed by a wind from the northeast. Later, there may be a cold rain.

Nadia shivers as she walks down to the shore. She turns naturally to the left and walks toward the farther point of land which forms the cove. Through the bare trees, she can see the cottages along her way, most of them now boarded up for the winter. She is barefoot, of course. I could lend her pants, a tee shirt and a baggy jacket, but my shoes would have been ridiculous on her, and would have damaged your image of Nadia. She is really quite beautiful with her dark hair, her dark complexion and the small mole on her cheek. In her present costume she looks innocent and waif-like.

We'll follow her about half way. She seems quite excited, stopping to pick up clamshells and collecting pelican feathers from the beach. She squints her eyes, looking for the glint off the lenses of binoculars, and imagining strange men huddled behind the buildings she passes. It occurs to her that this might be dangerous, and she feels a thrill of delicious fear. After all, there has been a murder. I seem relatively safe and gentle to her, but the circumstances of her arrival are strange, to say the least, and it is still too early for her to really tell about me. She has decided to wait until I fall asleep tonight, then read the story I am writing. Unfortunately, the story will still be incomplete, and she will not learn very much. I'll leave you sitting on a rock watching Nadia's slim figure disappear down the beach. I have to get back to my typewriter at the table in my cottage. There are a lot of loose ends I've got to tie together. I made quite a few promises in that first paragraph.

A lot has happened during that last brief digression. There has been a revolution in a tiny middle-east sheikdom. In a ruthless bid for power, one of my ex-students, now a major in his country's army, has taken over the sheikdom and put to death the entire royal family. Nobody knows what his politics are, and since a large percentage of the West's petroleum comes from his country, it is important that he be convinced of the nobility of our motives and of our willingness to pay. The Russians, of course, are hoping that he will favour them. He has announced that he will speak to only two people: me as representative of the West; and a certain Colonel Gregorov from the Soviet Union. A plane is waiting to fly me to the Middle East.

I'm going to have to count on you to take care of Nadia until I get back. I'll leave a note on the cottage door to that effect. You'll remember that there is every likelihood that this story will be read by young people, and I'll expect a certain decorum. I've already had my last book banned, and I don't want that to happen again. Adventure is fine, even a little romance, but nothing very explicit, please.

The plane trip was boring. They always are. We were met at the airport by a jeep and driven through the winding streets, past mosques with minarets. Peasants led donkeys laden with produce, and the streets were crowded with Arab traders. Everywhere, we saw women dressed in black, their faces modestly veiled. It didn't take me long to convince my ex-student where his real interests lay. I'd read a few stories he'd written and never published, so I knew the nature of his fantasy, and I also knew that certain relationships he'd had, though now over, still held him in ways he could hardly admit. Colonel Gregorov was furious. He caught up to me on our way out of the palace, and slipped me some not very veiled threats. He mentioned Nadia, of course, but it wasn't certain how much he knew. I suspected he wanted me to think he knew more than he did.

I was almost sick with worry when I got back. I'd been gone for over forty-eight hours, and the message was still pinned to the door. There was no sign of you or Nadia, and when I entered, I saw that the cottage had been ransacked. Everything was upside down. The cushions on the chairs had all been slit, pictures had been taken off the walls, the floor was littered with papers. Perhaps most suspicious of all, however, was this story, still sitting neatly beside the typewriter, the last half-finished page in the machine. It was clear that whoever had entered had read it. I flipped through the pages to see if there was any information that might help them, and I came on a paragraph I don't remember writing. It was back a few pages, and it was written in a beautiful imitation of my style, or at least I assume it was an imitation. I might have written the paragraph myself though, as I said, I don't remember doing so.

Suddenly, you and Nadia burst into the room holding hands. You are flushed and out of breath. You both begin talking at once. "It was terrible," Nadia begins. "You wouldn't believe," you say at the same moment, and I have to ask you to calm down and speak to me one at a time. You are still holding hands, but you become aware of this and of my presence as observer at the same time. You blush and separate.

You begin, and Nadia watches you with worshipful eyes. You had watched Nadia from your rock until she disappeared around the point of land. When after ten minutes she had not returned, you followed her steps. Just around the point you came on the signs of a struggle. The sand had been scuffed, you say, a torn piece of Nadia's baggy jacket was caught on a piece of driftwood, there were a few drops of blood. You ran up from the shore and you saw a white van driving away.

Nadia interjects again. "It was terrible. There were three men. They grabbed me and tied my hands and feet with a piece of rope. They tore a strip from the jacket and stuffed it into my mouth." She is panting from her memory of the exertion.

"I followed them," you continue. "They drove to another cottage about a block away." You sneaked around the back and hid in a shed. Then your concern for Nadia became so great that you dared to come right up to the window and peer in. Nadia lay on the floor, her hands and feet bound. The three men were sitting around the table drinking whiskey and talking in earnest tones. One of them

111

looked directly at the window.

"Did he see you?" I ask.

"No, it was as if he couldn't see me at all," you reply. And that makes sense. How could they have seen you, there in your armchair or on your seat in the bus.

"I couldn't go to the police," you tell me. "The men may have been the police themselves, or else the police may not have believed my story. So I waited until dark. Then, when two of the men left, I took a piece of stovewood from a pile in the yard. I knocked on the door, and when the third man answered, I struck him on the head with the stick of stovewood. He didn't even see me."

"Then he untied me," Nadia goes on. "We ran for what seemed like miles. Finally, we broke into a cottage through a back window. We've been there until just now, huddled under the covers in a bed because of the cold." She blushes.

"Finally," you say, "we took a chance and came here."

"Did you...?" I ask. I, too, am embarassed. This is not what I intended. You both nod and move closer together.

"Did anyone see you?" I ask.

"No," you reply, "they couldn't have. And yet all the time we were there I had the uncomfortable feeling we were being watched, like someone reading over your shoulder."

"About the man you struck," I ask. "Describe him to me."

Nadia answers. "He was in his early thirties. He looked Arab, and was wearing a three-piece pin-striped suit, and black oxfords. The odd thing about him was that he was wearing white socks."

Suddenly I remember. I ruffle through my papers and find an early draft. There is the exact description of the body, only it is lying on the beach, and sand is sticking to the hair. It is the paragraph I discovered inserted into the story when I returned from the Middle East. Beyond that, I realize now that it is the body of my student, the one who led the bloody revolution.

Then, there is a knock on the door. Nadia opens it and shouts, "Natashya!" The girl who stands in the doorway is identical in every respect to Nadia. They fall into each other's arms. She is, of course, Nadia's sister. She explains that she is fleeing from her jealous

112

husband, a certain Colonel Gregorov. I am bewildered.

"I was very young when I married," Natashya explains. "Nadia and I were inseparable as children, and when we were seventeen, our parents decided that our closeness was not healthy. I was sent to school in Switzerland."

"Lucerne," I say, "they sent you to Lucerne."

"Yes," she replies. "I didn't think you'd recognize me. Teachers don't always remember their students. I've changed a lot. Anyway, I met a young man there, an Arab by the name of Ibn Ben Said. He was wonderfully romantic, and he swept me off my feet. Only later, after we had eloped to Russia where he joined the Soviet army and changed his name to Gregorov, did I find out the truth about him. He was a man of insane jealousy. There was another man," she said, looking significantly at me, "with whom I would have been much better off, but I was too young to understand. Instead, I chose a man who insisted on wearing white socks on every occasion, and I've regretted that choice since. I hope it's not too late."

So here we are. I have my Natashya and you have your Nadia. I swear that on the first night she arrived, rolled in her carpet, nothing untoward occurred, no more than when you waited those hours in that cottage in front of a roaring fire. I know you did not huddle in bed, that your love was too pristine for such casual relationships. I haven't explained the carpet, but must everything be explained? Surely you can figure that out yourself. You are no fool. As for the spy, he did run for school board, and he won, putting spying behind him forever. For private reasons we are pleased that he is now on the school board, and we support him for chairman. We are happy now, the four of us in our elemental bliss, and the only one that sulks is that other out there, reading over your shoulder, searching for a moral that should be perfectly clear.

Sylvie

Sylvie says she loves me, but I believe she lies. She hasn't been to see me since the last day in July. That would be the thirty-first, and here it is into September. I know it's a busy season, all that cotton to pick, all them bales to tote, but you'd think she could bring me a little water every little once in a while. I don't think it's asking too much as a proof of love.

Sylvie claims she's been out of town, modelling in front of fountains in Rome, sitting on the walls of ruined castles along the Rhine, dressed in the newest styles. Tweeds are in, she tells me. There's a fortune to be made in tweeds. Put all your money into tweeds. What about cotton, I ask her, what about her Mammy and her Pappy and all her brothers and sisters down there in good ol' Alabam. Cotton's out, she says. Pappy, that slackass old bastard, ain't gonna make a penny on cotton. It's gonna be a lean winter down on the farm, now that tweed is in.

Pappy's been complaining about the moonshine, I tell her. He's been sending me letters complaining he can't get no moonshine. Sylvie says she sent him a gallon of Remy Martin. He just pigs it down, she says. Them people live like animals, she says. You can't do nuthin for them.

Sylvie phones me from Paris. She's modelling tweeds on the left bank. I'm drying for water, I tell her. Bring me little water, Sylvie, I say. You got running water, she tells me. Get yourself a glass and walk on over to the kitchen sink. Sylvie says she loves me. This can't be true, I tell her. If she really loved me, she'd have come to see me. I point out that she hasn't been to see me since the last day in July. I got a job, she says. I'm a working girl. We'll spend the Christmas holidays skiing at Banff.

I dream of Sylvie. I dream of Sylvie in my arms, Sylvie bringing me water. Sylvie doesn't dream of me. She says she can't dream. I say she could dream if she wanted, it's not that she can't dream, she won't dream. I want to be in Sylvie's dreams. I tell her if she just gives me a chance, I'll be wonderful in her dreams. I'll bring her pleasure free from guilt. I've promised if she dreams of me I'll take her to verdant glades. Sylvie says there weren't no verdant glades back in old Alabam. Nuthin but them old cotton fields back home.

I've sent Sylvie two heart-shaped lockets. One is blue and says *All Love Sylvie*. The other's red and says *Sylvie Loves All*. I got her two eighteen-carat gold chains to hang them around her neck. I told her I was so hot and dry that a little drink of water wouldn't satisfy me. Sylvie sent me a postcard from Copenhagen. The picture showed Sylvie in tweed posing in front of a fountain. She said she loved me. I'm not sure she's telling the truth. She hasn't been to see me since the last day in July.

I've got this tune running through my head. It goes, "Oh for Friday nicht, Friday's lang a-coming." That's all I can remember. There's got to be more words but I can't think of them. If Sylvie were here, she'd know them. She knows the words to all the songs. I run down to the supermarket and buy all the ladies' magazines. They all have pictures of Sylvie dressed in tweeds, posing in front of water fountains. Little drink of water, wouldn't satisfy me.

Kissing Sylvie is the best thing. Sylvie has a wonderful mouth. The first time she kissed me, we were only friends saying goodbye. Her mouth was red and sweet, and fresh. I couldn't think of anything else for days. The next time I kissed her, I asked her to marry me. Sylvie said she loved me, but she wouldn't marry me, only because she was already married.

Sylvie likes sandwiches, those little cocktail sandwiches that you pop into your mouth whole. She loves chocolates, the round sweet ones with a cherry in the centre. She pops them into her mouth. She drinks from long straws, pursing her mouth and looking up at you with wide open eyes. Sylvie pops raspberries and strawberries into her mouth. She bites deeply into peaches and pears, and doesn't care if the juice drips She bites into the red skin of apples and the orange flesh of oranges. Her kisses are sweet.

Sylvie sends me a telegram from Scotland. She says she is posing in tweeds in front of waterfalls. She has seen her husband, she says. That sucker isn't worth a pinch of peppered coonshit, she tells me. Sylvie says she loves me. She will be home Friday. I send Sylvie a telegram. I tell her, Oh for Friday nicht, Friday's lang a-coming. Bring me little water, Sylvie. Every little once in a while.

Sylvie's Pappy phones me up. We done run out of moonshine, boy, he tells me. Sure is hot down on them cotton fields without any moonshine. That Remy Martin weren't hardly enough to raise a thirst. I send him a gallon of Dewar's Ne Plus Ultra. I pass on Sylvie's message. Get out of cotton, old man. Tweed is in. Put all your money into tweed.

Sylvie phones me from Newfoundland. She's posing in tweeds on a fishing boat out in them old squid jigging grounds. She's a little tipsy from drinking screech. Put them fishermen in a cotton field, she says, and you couldn't tell the difference. That screech is great moonshine, she says. She's sending a gallon to her Pappy. I tell her she hasn't been to see me since the last day in July. I'll be home on Friday, she says.

I dream of Sylvie with her black, black hair, her black, black eyes. Sylvie doesn't dream of me. Let me into your dreams, I tell her. I'm a good man in a dream. I'm kind and gentle. I can bring you joy. Sorry, Sylvie says, I can't dream. I think she could dream if she wanted to. I believe she lies.

Sylvie's coming on Friday nicht, but Friday's lang a-coming. I'm getting ready. I've bought her peaches and cherries, strawberries and raspberries, oranges and bright red apples. I've bought her ice

117

cream and syrup and long thin straws so she can look up at me with her eyes wide open. I've bought her large bright cotton bibs, so the juice of peaches and pears won't drip on her tweed suit. I've bought her paper napkins with pictures of elves on them, so she can wipe her mouth when she's through. I've bought her a new heart-shaped locket with an eighteen-carat gold chain. When you look at it from a distance, it's blue, but when you look at it close up, it's red.

Sylvie says she loves me. Tomorrow will be Friday, and Sylvie's coming home. I'll kiss her in the airport, and I'll kiss her in the taxi and I'll feed her strawberries when we get home. Tonight I'll dream about her, and maybe she'll dream about me. I'm a good man in a dream. Bring me little water, Sylvie. I'll feed you raspberries and peaches and pears. You can drink from a long thin straw and look up at me from your wide, black eyes. Bring it in a bucket, Sylvie. Bring it in a bucket, now.

Point on a Line

Point on a line, Watson said to himself, unsure what he meant or where those words were likely to take him. *Pointona line, Poynto naline, poy unt uh na ly un.* It didn't help. The green 1966 Chevrolet Biscayne he was driving made a left turn onto a country road. The road looked familiar, but Watson couldn't identify it. Perhaps Angela lived on this road, Angela of the days of wine and roses, days of wine and roses, *daze uv wy nan droses.*

Listen, young feller. This is just a bit of advice, and I want you to understand it's only advice, see. Now you been hangin round our Angela, we know, hangin round trying to diddle our Angela with her golden hair and her lovely peach bright bosoms. Now see here, boy, we ain't gonna stand for that, no sir, nosirree. My suggestion to you boy is hop on your pony and ride, make tracks, get outta town quick like a bunny. I hope I make myself clear.

It was spring. There were apple blossoms. All along the road were apple orchards and the wind had scattered the blossoms so the road was covered with white petals. Point on a line, Watson whispered to himself. The Chevy swung around a curve in the road, and Watson peered through the window into a farmyard, looking for Angela.

She wasn't there, but a little girl was skipping rope in front of the barn.

You still hangin round here fella? You still trying to diddle our Angela with her cheeks like roses and the dainty spring in her step? I thought I warned you, boy. I thought I made myself perfectly clear. We don't want you moonin about, listenin for the lilt in our Angela's voice, watchin for the twinkle in her bottle-green eyes. Now move it, sucker, or you ain't gonna live to see daybreak, and your poor momma's gonna be weepin for her boy. Why don't you just think about your poor momma and move your ass outta here?

A little further down the road a sign pointed to a trail that led through the apple orchards. It said, ANGELA'S PLACE THREE MILES. Watson swung the Chevy down the narrow trail. Apple blossoms fell like rain, plastering themselves onto the green Chevy, covering the windshield so that Watson had to turn on his windshield wipers. Point on a line, he sang to himself, point on a line. Brightly coloured pheasants lined the sides of the trail. Sometimes they walked across the road so that Watson had to slow the Chevy to a crawl.

You did it, boy. Spite of all our warnings you went and diddled our Angela. Stole her maidenhood what was reserved for local community use. You took her roughly in the pride of her maiden innocence. You broke the hearts of several upstandin citizens that had their hearts set on makin Angela their legal wedded wife. And now, boy, you gonna pay. Me and Jed and Harry and the rest of these boys, we gonna take you for a little ride, and you can cancel all reservations. You ain't gonna need no more reservations.

Point on a line, sang Watson in his joy as the windshield wipers hammered out their percussive accompaniment. Point on a line. The trail ended at a tiny cottage, white with red trim and a red roof. It was surrounded by roses and vines with green leaves. White morning glories climbed all the way to the roof and surrounded the windows. A dainty hand-painted sign over the door said, ANGELA'S PLACE. The yard was white with apple blossoms, as if it had snowed.

Lissen, officer, this boy done soiled our Angela. He besmirched her reputation. He came in here with his fancy city clothes and his city talk and he swept that poor innocent girl offa her feet. Then he roont her. We ain't near half finished with him yet. He got some teeth we ain't smashed yet, and some bones in powerful need of breakin. And you boy? We ain't but half done with you, and iff'n you sets foot in this county again, we gonna finish the job. We takes pride in our work, boy, and a half-finished job don't set right with us.

Point on a line, Watson whispered under his breath. The door to the cottage opened, and Angela stepped out. Her golden hair haloed her face, and her breasts swelled under her long white nightgown. She took Watson by the hand and led him to a bower. She cradled him in her arms and sang to him. Birds gathered in the trees, and their twittering melded with the gentle murmur of the soft wind through the branches. The sunlight diffused through an easy mist.

You a damn lucky fella I happened by. Them boys play for keeps. Now I ain't got no sympathy for you city boys. What you did to our Angela deserves what you was gettin, but I got a job to do and I'm gonna do it. I'm droppin you off at the county line, and if you decide to complain, well you just might get yourself killed escapin lawful custody. Hear, boy? Spit that blood out the window and answer me.

Point on a line, Watson whispered to Angela. She looked at him out of her wide green eyes and stroked his face. Cherubs appeared in the upper left corner of the frame. I know, she sang to him in her lilting voice, every point on a line, every single point. She held him tightly as they ascended up through the branches and out of the frame, taking with them the birds, the cherubs, the breeze and the blossoms. All they left were the roses and a small pool of blood that widened until it covered the grass, the houses and the trees, and finally filled the entire frame.

A Girl's Story

You've wondered what it would be like to be a character in a story, to sort of slip out of your ordinary self and into some other character. Well, I'm offering you the opportunity. I've been trying to think of a heroine for this story, and frankly, it hasn't been going too well. A writer's life isn't easy, especially if, like me, he's got a tendency sometimes to drink a little bit too much. Yesterday, I went for a beer with Dennis and Ken (they're real-life friends of mine) and we stayed a little longer than we should have. Then I came home and quickly mixed a drink and starting drinking it so my wife would think the liquor on my breath came from the drink I was drinking and not from the drinks I had had earlier. I wasn't going to tell her about those drinks. Anyway, Wayne dropped over in the evening and I had some more drinks, and this morning my head isn't working very well.

To be absolutely frank about it, I always have trouble getting characters, even when I'm stone cold sober. I can think of plots; plots are really easy. If you can't think of one, you just pick up a book, and sure enough, there's a plot. You just move a few things around and nobody knows you stole the idea. Characters are the problem. It doesn't matter how good the plot is if your characters are dull. You can steal characters too, and put them into different plots. I've done that. I stole Eustacia Vye from Hardy and gave her another name. The problem was that she turned out a lot sulkier than I remembered and the plot I put her in was a light comedy. Now nobody wants to publish the story. I'm still sending it out, though. If you send a story to enough publishers, no matter how bad it is, somebody will ultimately publish it.

For this story I need a beautiful girl. You probably don't think you're beautiful enough, but I can fix that. I can do all kinds of retouching once I've got the basic material, and if I miss anything, Karl (he's my editor) will find it. So I'm going to make you fairly tall, about five-foot eight and a quarter in your stocking feet. I'm going to give you long blonde hair because long blonde hair is sexy and virtuous. Black hair can be sexy too, but it doesn't go with virtue. I've got to deal with a whole literary tradition where black-haired women are basically evil. If I were feeling better I might be able to do it in an ironic way, then black hair would be okay, but I don't think I'm up to it this morning. If you're going to use irony, then you've got to be really careful about tone. I could make you a redhead, but redheads have a way of turning out pixie-ish, and that would wreck my plot.

So you've got long blonde hair and you're this tall slender girl with amazingly blue eyes. Your face is narrow and your nose is straight and thin. I could have turned up the nose a little, but that would have made you cute, and I really need a beautiful girl. I'm going to put a tiny black mole on your cheek. It's traditional. If you want your character to be really beautiful there has to be some minor defect.

Now, I'm going to sit you on the bank of a river. I'm not much for setting. I've read so many things where you get great long descriptions of the setting, and mostly it's just boring. When my last book came out, one of the reviewers suggested that the reason I don't do settings is that I'm not very good at them. That's just silly. I'm writing a different kind of story, not that old realist stuff. If you think I can't do setting, just watch.

There's a curl in the river just below the old dam where the water seems to make a broad sweep. That flatness is deceptive, though. Under the innocent sheen of the mirroring surface, the current is treacherous. The water swirls, stabs, takes sharp angles and dangerous vectors. The trees that lean from the bank shimmer with the multi-hued greenness of elm, oak, maple and aspen. The leaves turn in the gentle breeze, showing their paler green undersides. The undergrowth, too, is thick and green, hiding the poison ivy, the poison sumac and the thorns. On a patch of grass that slopes gently to the water, the only clear part of the bank on that side of the river, a girl sits, a girl with long blonde hair. She has slipped a ring from her finger and seems to be holding it toward the light.

You see? I could do a lot more of that, but you wouldn't like it. I slipped a lot of details in there and provided all those hints about strange and dangerous things under the surface. That's called foreshadowing. I put in the ring at the end there so that you'd wonder what was going to happen. That's to create suspense. You're supposed to ask yourself what the ring means. Obviously it has something to do with love, rings always do, and since she's taken it off, obviously something has gone wrong in the love relationship. Now I just have to hold off answering that question for as long as I can, and I've got my story. I've got a friend who's also a writer who says never tell the buggers anything until they absolutely have to know.

I'm going to have trouble with the feminists about this story. I can see that already. I've got that river that's calm on the surface and boiling underneath, and I've got those trees that are gentle and beautiful with poisonous and dangerous undergrowth. Obviously, the girl is going to be like that, calm on the surface but passionate underneath. The feminists are going to say that I'm perpetuating stereotypes, that by giving the impression the girl is full of hidden passion I'm encouraging rapists. That's crazy. I'm just using a literary convention. Most of the world's great books are about the conflict between reason and passion. If you take that away, what's left to write about?

So I've got you sitting on the riverbank, twirling your ring. I forgot the birds. The trees are full of singing birds. There are meadowlarks and vireos and even Blackburnian warblers. I know a lot about birds but I'm not going to put in too many. You've got to be careful not to overdo things. In a minute I'm going to enter your mind and reveal what you're thinking. I'm going to do this in the third person. Using the first person is sometimes more effective, but I'm always afraid to do a female character in the first person. It seems wrong to me, like putting on a woman's dress.

Your name is Linda. I had to be careful not to give you a biblical name like Judith or Rachel. I don't want any symbolism in this story. Symbolism makes me sick, especially biblical symbolism. You always end up with some crazy moral argument that you don't believe and none of the readers believe. Then you lose control of your characters, because they've got to be like the biblical characters. You've got this terrific episode you'd like to use, but you can't because Rachel or Judith or whoever wouldn't do it. I think of stories with a lot of symbolism in them as sticky.

Here goes.

Linda held the ring up toward the light. The diamond flashed rainbow colours. It was a small diamond, and Linda reflected that it was probably a perfect symbol of her relationship with Gregg. Everything Gregg did was on a small scale. He was careful with his money and just as careful with his emotions. In one week they would have a small wedding and then move into a small apartment. She supposed that she ought to be happy. Gregg was very handsome, and she did love him. Why did it seem that she was walking into a trap?

That sounds kind of distant, but it's supposed to be distant. I'm using indirect quotation because the reader has just met Linda, and we don't want to get too intimate right away. Besides, I've got to get a lot of explaining done quickly, and if you can do it with the character's thoughts, then that's best.

Linda twirled the ring again, then with a suddenness that surprised her, she stood up and threw it into the river. She was immediately struck by a feeling of panic. For a moment she almost decided to dive into the river to try to recover it. Then, suddenly, she felt free. It was now impossible to marry Gregg. He would not forgive her for throwing the ring away. Gregg would say he'd had enough of her theatrics for one lifetime. He always accused her of being a romantic. She'd never had the courage to admit that he was correct, and that she intended to continue being a romantic. She was sitting alone by the river in a long blue dress because it was a romantic pose. Anyway, she thought a little wryly, you're only likely to find romance if you look for it in romantic places and dress for the occasion.

Suddenly, she heard a rustling in the bush, the sound of someone coming down the narrow path from the road above.

I had to do that, you see. I'd used up all the potential in the relationship with Gregg, and the plot would have started to flag if I hadn't introduced a new character. The man who is coming down the path is tall and athletic with wavy brown hair. He has dark brown eyes that crinkle when he smiles, and he looks kind. His skin is tanned, as if he spends a lot of time outdoors, and he moves gracefully. He is smoking a pipe. I don't want to give too many details. I'm not absolutely sure what features women find attractive in men these days, but what I've described seems safe enough. I got all of it from stories written by women, and I assume they must know. I could give him a chiselled jaw, but that's about as far as I'll go.

The man stepped into the clearing. He carried an old-fashioned wicker fishing creel and a telescoped fishing rod. Linda remained sitting on the grass, her blue dress spread out around her. The man noticed her and apologized.

"I'm sorry, I always come here to fish on Saturday afternoons and I've never encountered anyone here before." His voice was low with something of an amused tone in it.

"Don't worry," Linda replied. "I'll only be here for a little while. Go ahead and fish. I won't make any noise." In some way she couldn't understand, the man looked familiar to her. She felt she knew him. She thought she might have seen him on television or in a movie, but of course she knew that movie and television stars do not spend every Saturday afternoon fishing on the banks of small, muddy rivers.

"You can make all the noise you want," he told her. "The fish in this river are almost entirely deaf. Besides, I don't care if I catch any. I only like the act of fishing. If I catch them, then I have to take them home and clean them. Then I've got to cook them and eat them. I don't even like fish that much, and the fish you catch here all taste of mud."

"Why do you bother fishing then?" Linda asked him. "Why don't you just come and sit on the riverbank?"

"It's not that easy," he told her. "A beautiful girl in a blue dress may go and sit on a riverbank any time she wants. But a man can only sit on a riverbank if he has a very good reason. Because I fish, I am a man with a hobby. After a hard week of work, I deserve some relaxation. But if I just came and sat on the riverbank, I would be a romantic fool. People would make fun of me. They would think I was irresponsible, and before long I would be a failure." As he spoke, he attached a lure to his line, untelescoped his fishing pole and cast his line into the water.

You may object that this would not have happened in real life, that the conversation would have been awkward, that Linda would have been a bit frightened by the man. Well, why don't you just run out to the grocery store and buy a bottle of milk and a loaf of bread? The grocer will give you your change without even looking at you. That's what happens in real life, and if that's what you're after, why are you reading a book?

I'm sorry. I shouldn't have got upset. But it's not easy you know. Dialogue is about the hardest stuff to write. You've got all those "he saids" and "she saids" and "he replieds." And you've got to remember the quotation marks and whether the comma is inside or outside the quotation marks. Sometimes you can leave out the "he saids" and the "she saids" but then the reader gets confused and can't figure out who's talking. Hemingway is bad for that. Sometimes you can read an entire chapter without figuring out who is on what side.

Anyway, something must have been in the air that afternoon. Linda felt free and open.

Did I mention that it was warm and the sun was shining?

She chattered away, telling the stranger all about her life, what she had done when she was a little girl, the time her dad had taken the whole family to Hawaii and she got such a bad sunburn that she was peeling in February, how she was a better water skier than Gregg and how mad he got when she beat him at tennis. The man, whose name was Michael (you can use biblical names for men as long as you avoid Joshua or Isaac), told her he was a doctor, but had always wanted to be a cowboy. He told her about the time he skinned his knee when he fell off his bicycle and had to spend two weeks in the hospital because of infection. In short, they did what people who are falling in love always do. They unfolded their brightest and happiest memories and gave them to each other as gifts.

Then Michael took a bottle of wine and a Klik sandwich out of his wicker creel and invited Linda to join him in a picnic. He had forgotten his corkscrew and he had to push the cork down into the bottle with his filletting knife. They drank wine and laughed and spat out little pieces of cork. Michael reeled in his line, and to his amazement discovered a diamond ring on his hook. Linda didn't dare tell him where the ring had come from. Then Michael took Linda's hand, and slipped the ring onto her finger. In a comic-solemn voice, he asked her to marry him. With the same kind of comic solemnity, she agreed. Then they kissed, a first gentle kiss with their lips barely brushing and without touching each other.

Now I've got to bring this to some kind of ending. You think writers know how stories end before they write them, but that's not true. We're wracked with confusion and guilt about how things are going to end. And just as you're playing the role of Linda in this story, Michael is my alter ego. He even looks a little like me and he smokes the same kind of pipe. We all want this to end happily. If I were going to be realistic about this, I suppose I'd have to let them make love. Then, shaken with guilt and horror, Linda would go back and marry Gregg, and the doctor would go back to his practice. But I'm not going to do that. In the story from which I stole the plot, Michael turned out not to be a doctor at all, but a returned soldier who had always been in love with Linda. She recognized him as they kissed, because they had kissed as children, and even though they had grown up and changed, she recognized the flavour of wintergreen on his breath. That's no good. It brings in too many unexplained facts at the last minute.

I'm going to end it right here at the moment of the kiss. You can do what you want with the rest of it, except you can't make him a returned soldier, and you can't have them make love then separate forever. I've eliminated those options. In fact, I think I'll eliminate all options. This is where the story ends, at the moment of the kiss. It goes on and on forever while cities burn, nations rise and fall, galaxies are born and die, and the universe snuffs out the stars one by one. It goes on, the story, the brush of a kiss.

Girl and Wolf

It is morning. The possibilities for the wolf are open and endless. The paths through the forest run in every direction. The pale green new leaves on the trees are welcome after a hard winter. The breeze is gentle and ruffles his fur. The wolf is hungry, he is always hungry. That is what it is to be a wolf. The wolf is sleek and limber. As he runs, he admires his own grace.

The red-haired girl is going to see her grandmother. The weather is the same for her, same morning, same breeze, same new green leaves. The girl is tall and well made. She has already forgotten all her mother's cautions. She is ready to talk to strangers, she is eager for strangers and adventures. A girl's life is surrounded by cautions, she is circumscribed by rules. Only a forest offers freedom.

The paths through the forest run in all directions. They meet and intersect. They double back on themselves, intertwine. There are a thousand nodes, a thousand crossings. At any one of these crossings the girl might encounter the wolf. There are so many crossings that it is inevitable that at one of them wolf and girl will meet.

When they meet, the wolf must ask the question, the girl must answer. Where are you going? To visit my grandmother. It is the question all wolves ask, the answer all girls give. The girl's path is the path of needles, the wolf will follow the path of pins. Needles and pins, the path leads to the grandmother's house, all paths lead to the grandmother's house.

The wolf is there first. He is always first. He runs with his easy gait down the winding path. The girl is distracted. She strays from the path, she picks flowers, she stops to drink at a stream. The wolf is early. He must wait for the girl. It is only the start of his waiting. The wolf eats the grandmother. He must pass the time somehow, and he is hungry. Even then—and that takes some time, the grandmother is old and stringy—he must wait. He lies in the bed.

The girl knocks at the door. The wolf, in the bed, is nearly mad with impatience. He is sick with desire. "Come in," he shouts. The girl enters. The girl likes entrances. She is fresh and perfumed from the flowers she has picked. She dances in the door, her dress swirls, her red hair swirls. "Grandmother," she says, "see, I have picked you some flowers."

"Bring them here," the wolf answers. She gets a glass of water from the kitchen. She puts the flowers in water and brings them to the bed. She knows that the wolf is not her grandmother. She recognizes him as the stranger she met in the forest. Still, she is calm. She seems to know what she is doing, or else she is caught by some force that makes her operate against her will.

"Come, get into the bed with me," the wolf tells the girl. It is a desperate ruse. If she recognizes him all will be lost. And how can she fail to recognize him? He is not even masked. All his life it has been like this. He is never properly prepared. He never has the disguise he needs, the mask he should wear.

"What shall I do with my coat?" she asks.

"Throw it in the fire," the wolf tells her. "You won't need it any more."

The girl takes off her coat and throws it into the fire. "And what shall I do with my dress?" she asks.

"Take it off and throw it into the fire. You won't need it any more."

She slips the dress over her head and throws it into the fire. She is wearing a white slip and red shoes. "What shall I do with my shoes?" she asks.

"Take them off and throw them into the fire. You won't be needing them any more."

The girl sits on the edge of the bed to take off her shoes. She bends with an awkwardness the wolf finds touching. She slips off one shoe at a time and throws them into the fire. "What shall I do with my slip?" she asks the wolf.

"Take it off and throw it into the fire. You won't be needing it any more." The girl pulls the slip over her head and throws it into the fire. She has on black panties and a black brassiere. Panties and brassiere are edged with lace. They look expensive.

"What shall I do with my brassiere?" the girls asks the wolf. Her red hair spills over the whiteness of her shoulders.

"Take it off and throw it into the fire. You won't be needing it any more." The wolf is tense. Is he perhaps too eager? He is trying to make his answers part of a ritual that will complete itself out of its inner necessity. One false step now, and the charm might be broken.

The girl takes off her brassiere and throws it into the fire. Her breasts spill out, or at least the only words that come to the wolf's mind are *spill out*. The girl's breasts are high and firm and very large. They accentuate the slimness of her waist. In the cool air of the room, her nipples grow firm.

"And what shall I do with my panties?"

"Take them off and throw them into the fire. You won't need them any more."

The girl slips down her panties and flips them into the fire with her toe. She stands there, entirely naked. The little triangle is a paler red than her hair. The girl gets into the bed and snuggles up against the wolf. Her hair seems even redder against the white of the sheets.

"Why do you have so much hair on your body, grandmother?" she asks. She rubs her hands along the wolf's body, and he feels rising in himself something that might have been hunger if he hadn't just eaten.

"It keeps me warm,"the wolf replies.

"And why do you have such large eyes?" she asks, and as she asks, she looks at him with her own wide green eyes.

"The better to see you with," the wolf says, though he knows the inadequacy of that answer. He can feel her firm breasts pressed against his body.

"And why do you have such large teeth?" she asks. It is his moment. The wolf knows there will be no more questions. Everything depends on his answer now. He hesitates a moment, but there is really no option. There is only one answer, and there has never really been a choice. He says it reluctantly. "The better to eat you with."

"Nonsense," the girl replies, sliding under the wolf and pulling him on top of her. Her hands slip down to his hindquarters, easing his entry. The girl likes entrances. The wolf moans in his delight, a moan that blends with the ecstatic moans of all his ancestors. The girl is inexperienced but active, and when it is over, the wolf doesn't know whether what he feels is joy or pain.

The girl lights a cigarette from a package on her grandmother's table. She sits cross-legged on the bed, looking at the wolf. "That was nice," she says. "We're going to get along fine." She blows the smoke out her nostrils and flicks some ashes onto the floor. "It's a pity about my clothes, though. I'm going to have to get an entire new wardrobe. You don't have a job, I know that, but it will all work out. You can work at my dad's service station until something better comes along."

Just then there is a knock at the door. The girl finds a robe in her grandmother's closet. She slips it over her nakedness and goes to the door. A woodcutter stands there, his axe gleaming in his hand.

"Is everything all right?" he asks.

"Just fine," the girl says.

"I was wondering about your grandmother."

"Grandma's gone to Tucson, Arizona, to live with my aunt," the girl tells him. She's given the house to me and my fiancé. We're going to be doing some renovating, so if you're looking for work, why don't you drop around in a couple of weeks."

The wolf already knows the ending. It is the last of his wolfhood. His morning runs down the winding and criss-crossing trails of the forest are over. Already, his legs ache from the concrete on which he will stand. His fur is beginning to smell of oil. And so it has always been. What is the good of cautioning young girls? Grandmothers cannot be trusted. They are always somewhere else. The woodcutter is always too late. Whatever is lost is lost forever, and the forest trails, though they wind and cross, are searching for somebody else's meetings.

The Circus Performers' Bar

I am the first of our group here tonight, alone at our table in the corner of the Circus Performers' Bar on Latayefsky street. I walked here along the canal in a fog that turned the streetlamps into blurs of gold and my fellow canal walkers into ghosts. It's an unusual winter in St. Petersburg, nearly the end of January and still no snow. Every day it rains, drizzle out of a grey sky.

Here in the Circus Performers' Bar, a fire blazes in the fireplace and the smell of fresh bread makes me think of my mother's kitchen in Vilnya. Perhaps this winter I will go back to visit the old folks, but I have been promising myself to make that journey for three years now, and always, something comes up to make it impossible. I'm sure it would be the same as it always is. First, there would be feasting and rejoicing over the return of the prodigal son, hugs and kisses everywhere, beer and sausages and sauerkraut. Then in a few days, their narrow peasant minds, filled with superstition and fear and petty malice, would begin to weigh on me. I would say something wrong, suggest perhaps that the Jew on the corner was as much a victim as they, and we would begin the inevitable argument, the argument that drove me from home when I was fifteen. My father

137

would shake his fist and curse me, and I would ride the dreadful train back to St. Petersburg, shaking with rage.

I am normally the last to arrive. I like to step into gaiety and good companionship after it is already ripe. I like to be a little less drunk than the others, the receiver rather than the giver of confidences. And I like to be the one that is responsible at the end to see that the others are got safely home with the correct scarves and mitts and hats. The others count on me to be the sober caretaker.

But tonight some heaviness of the spirit drove me from my room on Svetlana street. All afternoon I felt restless, neither my beloved Shakespeare nor my equally beloved Flaubert could settle me. I, who love so much to be alone, could not bear my solitary company, and I fled into the street. I should have gone to the performance of the Boukevenian dancers at the Palace of the Arts. Afterwards, I might have joined them for supper, plied some savage mountain girl with vodka and wit, and taken her back to my room. We could have made love intensely; I am not an acrobat for nothing.

That's what I should have done. Instead, I sat on the bridge near the railway station, watching the thick dirty water curl beneath me until I was chilled and hurried here. Now I sit, sipping my Pernod and watching my fellow performers straggle in. Leuba Romanovna, our fat lady, sits in her special chair, where she stays all day long, drinking oceans of beer and eating tiny dainty sandwiches. She lives in a room at the back of the bar, and every day she spreads herself out by the window to watch the people walk past. Sometimes the prostitutes from the street come in to join her for a few minutes, just to get warm, but most of the time she is silent and alone. At the next table, Pyotr Petrovich drinks in his bitter rage. No one ever sits with him. Sometimes, he hires a prostitute and is gone for an hour or so, but this is not very often, because the prostitutes know him. He beats them, and they demand very high pay for his pleasure. He is a mean and hurtful man, but the children love him in his clown's costume with his bright red nose. Then he is all sunshine and warmth. It's as if the goodness in him were drained from his body by his performances, leaving only rage.

The animal handlers have already gathered at their table, telling coarse jokes and complaining because they must care for the animals in the winter, while the rest of us live our ordinary lives. There are always a few gawkers, hoping to get a bit of a free show, but they are always disappointed because in ordinary street clothing even the freaks look like anybody else. Ilya the Fish Man has covered his scales with a black suit and looks like a butcher's boy with a bad complexion. Mitka the Three-Legged Man looks like any other cripple.

But now, look, the door has swung open and in comes Taras Zarnytsyn, the Captain, with his broad chest and his cavalry officer's beard. "Let the revels begin!" he shouts, and he throws his dwarf's body forward in a high, arching flip that lands him in the centre of the room. The gawkers applaud. This is what they came to see. The Captain claps his hands. "Marfa, Dounia, bring me wine, bring me sausage, bring me the blood of princes. Tonight the Captain celebrates."

"A song, Captain," somebody shouts, and the others take it up. "A song, Captain, give us a song." With a bound, the Captain is up on a table, and the room fills with his rich baritone. He sings a song of love, a song of spring. Deep in the mountains a maiden weeps for her lover, a dashing cavalry officer. On a distant plain, the ravens peck the eyes from a dead soldier. Every eye in the room fills with tears, weeping for lost love and the inevitability of death. Then, suddenly, the cavalry officer comes back to claim the maiden. It was not he who lay dead on the plain, but his enemy. The room fills with laughter and shouts. The Captain might have been an opera singer, one of the finest in all Russia. But the people who go to operas will not listen to a dwarf, and so he is an acrobat in the Circus of the Western Region. The crowd cries for more. No one likes a fine performance more than a circus performer does, but the Captain bows graciously and joins me at our table.

"Ah, Dmitri," he teases, "you are early. Come to negotiate with the prostitutes before they raise their fees for the evening?"

I feel my face redden. Like everyone else, I feel inferior when alone with the Captain. His energy and good will are so intense that it seems like some special favour he bestows when he directs his attention to you.

139

"I have sent my proof of Fermat's theorem to Paris," I tell him, feeling like a schoolboy. I have a letter from *Le Journal des Mathématiques Spéciales*, and if the mathematicians of Paris cannot find a flaw, they will publish it.

"Good, good," he says, not understanding the importance of what I have told him. I know too that I have just broken the unwritten rule of the troupe. We may speak of our lusts and desires, our inner fears, but we may not speak of our talent. The Captain will not tell me of his humiliations at the opera house. I know he still goes to auditions, though he is never chosen. I should not tell him of my mathematics, or at least I should only tell him of success, and the letter, while encouraging, is not yet success.

Before we can begin again, this time keeping the conversation at the level of banter where it belongs, Ivan, Lev and Carl arrive, and they have in tow a young girl. Ivan, with a sweeping bow, introduces her as Sonia. She has the whitest skin I have ever seen, and her hair is jet black. Hers is the kind of beauty you never get to study, but only see passing quickly on a crowded street. I can see that Ivan, Lev and Carl are already in love with her, and I know that in a very few minutes I will be too. I groan aloud, foreseeing weeks of hopeless yearning, futile attempts to turn myself into something that might attract her, knowing even at this moment when I haven't yet fallen in love that there is no magic in this world strong enough to transform me into what I would have to become.

Lev, the poet among us, runs to the kitchen, calling for Marva and Dounia. I can hear him telling them that no, sausage will not do, she must have a chicken. Lev has had many of his poems published in the journals, though he has never met another writer or an editor. His poems are strange tales of giants, men from some remote tribe in the Urals who are kind to their children and wives, and who defeat their enemies. Lev is a Jew.

Sonia leans across the table to Ivan telling him, no, no, it is too much, there is no need. He answers her, putting on the Moscow accent of his youth, that she need not worry, it is but a trifle. Ivan is an engineer and he constructs his sentences like bridges. He is the only one of us who was not driven from his home by an angry father, who

140

was never beaten. He need not be an acrobat. He could work with his father in Moscow, the father who loves him, who comes to see our performances and weeps.

Carl whispers to me that they found her on the outskirts of the city. She had been wandering lost in the forest. A hunter had discovered her and out of pity was taking her home, but he had feared that his wife would not understand, and so had asked for their help. They know nothing of her except that her lover has been imprisoned by the czar. She was going to meet him, to live outside the camp and visit him on Sundays, but she had no money. The conductor of the train had let her ride as long as he dared, but she had to leave when the soldiers came. She had lost her way then, and wandered for hours until the hunter found her. Carl wants to paint her. He will pay her to model for him until she has enough money to buy another ticket, and who knows, maybe she will forget about her lover in his prison.

We are done for, all of us, I can see that now. The street girls, the prostitutes, the lonely farm girls just arrived in the city were some compensation for the brutal joke played on us by nature and our fathers. But this girl of blood and milk with her black hair, black eyes, white skin and red lips will teach us what we are: stunted inadequate parodies of men leaping up to try to touch the moon. Lev is back with the chicken and a goblet of white wine, and we try to counterfeit a gaiety that will disguise the yearning that hangs heavy over our table at the Circus Performers' Bar.

The Captain is teasing her now, telling her that she must join the circus. He tells her that he will buy her six white horses, the most beautiful horses in all of Russia. She will dance on the backs of the horses as they circle round and round the ring, and the crowd will cheer and cry, "Sonia, Sonia." She laughs, and her laughter tinkles like bells. Her black eyes sparkle as she teases him back, saying she would be happier with one small pony she could ride in a lonely field. We glow with her approval.

And now suddenly I see that Nikolai and Rodya are in the room, slipping from table to table whispering something that turns each table to excited conversation. Rodya is our carpenter. When his hands touch wood it takes on the shape he desires. All our clubs and hoops, our bars and horses come from his hands. It is strange that he and Nikolai should be the closest friends, because they are so different. Nikolai is our leader, the disciplinarian who designs our pyramids, who coaches us through the endless hours of practice, tumbling and juggling until our routine is perfect. He is an anarchist, and in every village of the Western Region, he attends secret, mysterious meetings.

Now they are at our table, bursting with such excitement that they scarcely notice Sonia. Never mind, there will be plenty of time for that.

"Gentlemen," Nikolai cries, "the new age is dawning. The shackles of the old are forever gone. The revolution has begun. The troops fired on Father Gapon and a hundred people are dead. Now the citizens are out in the streets in Moscow and soon the entire country will be in a fire that will burn away the old. This Sunday of blood will live forever." We stare at him in amazed disbelief. "Think of it," he goes on, "you Dmitri, will teach at the University. The Captain will sing at the State Opera. Carl, your paintings will hang on every wall."

"And the prisoners," Sonia asks him, "what will become of the prisoners?"

"Already they are being freed everywhere. The new Russia will have no need of prisons."

Nikolai leans over to talk intensely with Sonia. Her cheeks are flushed with excitement. Whatever shape the new world takes, there will be room in it for her. However it is made, it will need princesses. But after this hour, nothing will ever make it whole for me. Here I sit, burning with love, aching with desire, stunted, dwarfed, and out in the street, already, the guns are beginning.

The Girl of Milk and Blood

Giorgio

The cold dry bora is blowing again, down from the east beyond the mountains. My face is cracked, like the clay bottoms of the stream beds after the fall rains have run off into the valley below. Each crack is a tiny portion of agony, and the relentless wind fills them with dust. The women rub their faces with butter to keep them smooth, and that is good enough for a walk to the well, or over to the neighbour's place to gossip in the afternoon, but it is of no help for a day spent on the side of the mountain. The cattle are always thirsty, as if the dryness of the wind had sucked the very moisture from their bodies.

It is on days like this that I think of my boyhood further east in the underground caves and streams of the karst. Deep in the limestone caves, there was only one season, a cool dark season of crystal water and candlelight at noon. When I joined the brotherhood, I never dreamed of this godforsaken mountain with its impoverished valley below. I knew nothing of the disastrous rains that can wipe out a village in an hour, or the kind of stubborn people who would gather up their surviving relatives and rebuild their village in the path of the same murderous flood. I never thought of snow ten metres deep, or this devil of a drying wind.

There is beauty here, all right, but it is a spare, cramped beauty, the beauty of twisted dwarf juniper and green alder and stunted rhododendron. In the spring, the snowdrops peep out from the melting snow, and later there are gentian and saxifrage, rock jasmine, campion and primrose. If your eyes are keen, you might see rabbits or partridges or grouse and, once in a very long time, a golden eagle or a mountain roe. For the rest, you must satisfy yourself with vipers, salamanders and newts. And this is fitting, I suppose, because this is a community without forgiveness. Here, no wrong is ever forgotten, no insult ever properly redressed, even by death. Revenge seeps up from the valley below like a poisonous fog, and it dries our souls as surely as the bora dries our skin.

Bellemondo is the name of our village, a name left over from some hopeful past, though nothing but an irony now. Our sister villages are Pontebba and Comegliano, but no one ever goes to them. Once in a while some enterprising villager will take the mountain roads down to Udine and catch the train to Trieste, perhaps to buy a wedding dress for a daughter or to present a government official with some bewildering request. In this village we speak Friulan, and in the valley below the farmers speak Slovene. Italian is a foreign language, spoken only by the odd official who blunders into our village, and by our mayor, who is mayor only because he can speak Italian. We of the brotherhood speak it, of course, but we are considered outsiders, though all seven of us have spent most of our lives here. In this village you can be an outsider for generations.

Our village sits at the foot of an old castle, where once a baron ruled in feudal splendour, though there has been no baron here for over a century. Now, the castle belongs to the Americans, who repaired the high walls that surround it, and who, for a couple of weeks each summer, arrive in their four-wheel-drive vehicles and disappear behind the wall. They bring everything they need, so that they never have to speak to a villager. Or they used to. Now the Germans have taken over, though they are almost as distant as the

144

Americans. Every few days a military vehicle drives through the town and down the winding road to Udine.

All we know of the war is that the Germans are in the castle. We of the brotherhood have a radio, and we follow the strange course of the war as if it were some extended game whose rules aren't clear, even to the players. But perhaps today we will learn more of it. Antonio, whose duty it is to listen to the radio, told me this morning that Marshall Badoglio has declared war on Germany. That means that the Germans, who were our friends, are now our enemies, and the mysterious people in the castle are now an occupying force. We are all encouraged to join the resistance, though so far there has been nothing to resist. We are told that the Germans are brutal, that they rape women and murder little children. Our women in their black shawls and black dresses with their rotten teeth are no great incitement to rape. They even tie handkerchiefs around their knees so that the sight of so much flesh will not unduly excite their husbands. Still, there are enough children around, though I sometimes wonder whether the joys of the flesh or the need for another hand in the fields is the chief inducement to lust in our village.

This year, I am in charge of the cattle. Each morning, I drive them high into the mountains to feed on the sparse grasses and at night I return them to their shed, which, as in every other house in our village, is directly below our living quarters. I look forward to the snows, when the cattle will have to stay in, and I will only have to throw them their hay and milk them. Then, through the long dark winter days I will play chess with Mario or Emilio, or one of the others whose work will not take him from the house. Last year I was the fisher and could spend my time in the cool of the forest under the beeches, the larch and the towering Norwegian spruces. I was clever at that, and I caught more brown trout and eels than we seven could eat. Sometimes I would even catch a sturgeon, and though the old ones speak of a time when sturgeon were plentiful, they are rare enough now. Next year I will be the carpenter, and though my hands are not good with wood, it will be better than sitting on the side of this mountain in the dry, cold wind that never, even for a moment, lets up.

Sandro

Giorgio tells me that something is happening at the castle. From the pasture in the mountains he can see over the walls into the court-yard. There is now a large black limousine parked with the army trucks. Someone important has come, though there is no gossip in the village. Whoever it is must have arrived at night with the convoy of trucks. He says he thinks he saw a woman in a white dress walk to the gate, then hurry back to the castle door, but he is a half mile away and it is unlikely he could have seen that. Herding the cattle is the worst job. There is nothing to do but sit, and sometimes the imagin-ation takes over. When it was my turn, I too saw strange things.

I think I may have made a very bad mistake. One of the drivers stopped his jeep and asked me the way to the castle. Without think-ing, I answered him in German. He seemed surprised, though he said nothing. It is difficult enough for a dwarf to escape notice without advertising his presence by speaking languages he should not speak. Gian Petro says that the time of our mission is near. I hope so. I have waited twenty years in this place, knowing only my own part of the mission and sworn not to tell or ask of the others' parts. On the day that Gian Petro gives the word that the mission must begin, then we shall all know. Now, even he knows only the signs that will release us to our acts.

Once again, the spring has failed. Gian Petro tells us that once this was the most fertile valley in all of Italy. In spring the vineyards on the slopes sprang into life and the air was so heavy with the fragrance of blossoms you were made dizzy by it. Then, he says, the cattle were fat and didn't have to be driven up into the mountains, because the grass was so lush that when they ate one blade, another leaped up to take its place. Then the air was heavy with bees, and a thousand different kinds of birds woke you with their singing every day. The peasants sang at their work, and there were festivals for every occasion, the Festival of the Spring Flowers, the Festival of the Jousting of the Queens, the Winemakers' Festival, the Festival of the Shoemakers' Guild and a hundred others.

146

Now, there are no festivals. The air itself seems to be poisoned. When the bora blows from the east, the leaves on trees shrivel and crack. When the clouds come in from the south, the rains wash away a whole summer's work. From the north come snows that bury us and untimely frosts that kill the young buds. Only the west wind brings us hope, but the wind is almost never from the west.

I have tended the vines with immaculate care, tying them into hearts as my father taught me to do at home in the Moselle valley, but where there should be a riot of leaves, there are only a few sickly buds. At home the wine was amber and tasted like honey. Here, I will produce once more a wine that is pale and sour. Only the vegetables that hide underground can survive, turnips, potatoes, carrots and parsnips.

Perhaps the Germans know that, and that is why they are searching all the houses. Three more truckloads came in today, large humourless men who surrounded all the houses in the village, then searched them from top to bottom. They found nothing, of course. The houses are all above ground. The few partisans we have are frightened young men who hide in the caves lower in the valley, and who have no weapons to oppose the occupiers.

Antonio

Listen. Through the spit and crackle of the radio set you can hear all the voices of Babel: French, German, Italian, English, Russian, Spanish, Dutch, Arabic, so many languages, so many lies being told. After each battle, all sides proclaim themselves winners, so much destroyed, so many killed, bridges blown up, factories exploded. They taunt each other in each other's language, they urge the people at home to sacrifice for final victory, so many glorious countries, so much fighting to preserve civilization from the maddened hordes outside.

After a while, you know them all, all the languages. They say the same things in the same rhythms so that you learn that meaning is not in the words but in the patterns, some grammar common to

147

them all for which the words are merely clothing. And somehow, somewhere in the gaps between what is said runs a thin line of truth, a delicate wavering line that breaks and rejoins, disappears into the welter of words, then reappears. This is the line I listen to, this thin band of silence which carries the current of events.

I have listened for so long now that I hardly need my other senses. I make my way home down the steep mountain path from my cave by the sound of the water rippling in a distant stream, the whistle of wind over rocks, the nodding and rustling of trees. I hear the earth's exhalations, the moisture in the earth being drawn upwards by the sun. As I approach the town, I hear the women roll over in their beds, I hear the men scratch themselves. I can hear the scurry of mice in attics, the spinning of spiders' webs, the grass growing and leaves unfurling. If I stand very still, I can hear into the hearts of atoms, the electrons swirling around their nuclei.

And so I know this war is nearly over. Through the radio's static I can hear the tanks moving upward from the south. Rome fell today, and I could hear the sounds of rejoicing in the streets. It will still be a while before the troops get this far north, and so we must be very careful. We are like a patient with an evil growth in the heart. We must be careful that the operation that removes that growth does not kill us all. I have warned the partisans to keep to their caves. Events larger than they are shaping history, and it is better they be alive to farm when this is over, than some one German car should be destroyed.

Someone is being held in the castle, someone who is more important than any single battle. Giorgio has seen her from the pasture above the castle, a woman in a white dress who is rarely allowed even into the grounds. I believe I can hear her weeping as I circle the castle on my way home from the listening cave. Von Ribbentrop himself has been to see her several times. He comes in the dead of the night and is gone again by morning. I thought perhaps she was his daughter, but I no longer think so. The radio from the castle reports in a code I cannot understand. It sounds like the random static you hear when there are sunspots.

148

They splish and they splash, these trout, they dance on their tails. When the weather is good, they are eager for the net. They say to each other, "Look, Guido is here again, we will tease him with our dancing, then when he is frantic with worry that he will catch nothing, we will swim into his net." The eels, they are another thing, the eels, they are evil. They glide so silently over the shallow beds of streams, they hide in the deep holes, they are like the snake that tempted poor Eve when she was all innocence and could not have known better. They eat birds, yes they do, those eels, they eat baby ducklings. The mother has a brood of ten, then in one silent swallow so that she does not even know it has happened, she has a brood of nine.

But worst of all is the dark one, Old Snapper, who hides in the depths of the deepest pools. Sometimes, you think you see a log, just below the surface something darker than the darkness of deep water, but when you see him, it is already too late, because he always sees you first and is gone. The others are all proud because they caught sturgeon, but they never caught Old Snapper, and what is the good of catching any other? I have caught them too, sturgeon I mean, but I have let them go. The trout are fine because they know they are food, and they like to be caught, and the eels are fine because they are evil and deserve to be eaten, but a sturgeon is no good unless he is Old Snapper, because every mouthful you eat reminds you that Old Snapper is still there, at the bottom of some pool, laughing at you.

It is going to be harder to catch him, now that winter has come and the snow is piled along the banks of the streams. In some places, there is ice, but the ice is treacherous. A German soldier fell through the ice, and if Old Snapper has not eaten him, he is at the bottom of a pool. In the spring he will rise and be tumbled down the stream until his clothing catches on to a root or a twig, and we will find him and take him to the priest to bury.

Old Snapper and the German soldier will have to wait until another day. Today I must catch trout. Since the girl of milk and blood has come to live with us, I must see that we have fresh trout every day. It was me who found her, little Guido who everyone pats on the head because I am happy and I sing. I took her from the woodcutter, who is a good man but full of fear. He found her wandering under the larches in her white robe with three drops of blood on her breast. Her eyes are the palest blue, and her long hair is so white that it looks silver. Her complexion is the colour of milk. The woodcutter says she escaped from the castle. She was terrified, and didn't want to go back. The woodcutter didn't know what to do. If the people from the castle caught him with the girl, they would kill him, and so he brought her to us, to me, little Guido. I took her to a cave that only I know, and lit a fire. Then when it was dark, I went for the others, and we carried her home wrapped in a blanket. Gian Petro says it is the start of our mission. We must protect her until other things come clear. That night, I was given an extra portion of the evening rum, then I sang a song for them, a song about a little bird that is pierced by a thorn, but who sings so beautifully that all the animals of the forest weep, until their tears become a river and a golden boat floats down the river with a handsome prince who rescues the little bird, who is really a princess. When I was finished, the girl of milk and blood kissed me on the forehead, and since then I have been so filled with joy, my heart is ready to burst.

She is good, the girl of milk and blood, so good that thinking of her goodness can bring any of us to tears. Her skin is so delicate that anything that touches it leaves a bruise. She says she must do her part in our household, and so she mends our clothes. Last night, a needle pricked her thumb and splattered three drops of blood onto her white robe, so that she was just as I found her. She fainted, and when she awoke, she could remember nothing, only that she is terrified of the castle. Gian Petro says it is a warning of danger. He says we must go about our business as if nothing had happened, and he has cautioned the girl of milk and blood not to open the door to any knock. I think if I could catch Old Snapper, the dark one, everything would work out right. I have mentioned this to the others, but they tell me that is nonsense. Still, I think I know how it can be done, not with a net, but with a line, and lure made from a piece of white cloth with three drops of blood.

Rico

Today my hands shake, the chisel turns and twists, making gouges in the wood. Gian Petro says I can have no day of rest, but must continue making sabots. We are in terrible danger, he says, and so we must go on as if nothing had happened or else our mission will be lost. I think it is lost already with the loss of the girl. We should never have tried to live our ordinary lives. We should have taken her to the deepest cave and hidden her away until it was safe. We have supplies sufficient for a year, and if the war still raged, we might spirit her away to the south, to freedom.

Now the house is still with an awful stillness. All that joy that bubbled through the house these last three months is gone. The walls seem still to hold the echo of her songs, and the ripple of her laugh hovers in the corner of the room. And still we have no idea who she was, no more idea than she had herself. She was like, not a new-born child, but a new-born woman. Her innocence was amazing, a purity so great it was palpable. Her hands were so delicate she could never have done a stitch of work in her life. And yet she learned, she learned so quickly. We would have done everything for her, but Gian Petro said, no, she was not a plaything. She would have to work for her keep like the rest of us.

And work she did. She darned our clothes and washed them cleaner than they had ever been. She swept the floor and made the beds and cooked our meals. At first, she had to be shown how to do the simplest things, how to thread a needle, how to hold a broom, how to start a fire. But once she had learned, she made us feel awkward and clumsy just watching her grace.

Her skin was so delicate that anything might bruise it, and she cut herself often. Then she would bleed, though never more than a few drops. Her cuts would heal miraculously in a day, but the bruises

151

lasted for weeks, tingeing the whiteness of her skin with blue. She cooked the most wonderful meals, but would eat nothing herself but a little milk and, occasionally, to please Guido, a mouthful of trout. She was frightened of the eels and refused to touch them. When Gian Petro insisted she cook them, I took a few moments away from my chisels and cooked them for her. It was a small deception.

The plants in our house are starting to droop, mourning for her, though I water them every day. When she arrived, they burst into a profusion of leaves, as if it were already spring. She spoke to them, encouraged the tiny buds, called white flowers out of plants that had never flowered before, white flowers with a touch of scarlet at the centre.

I wept while I made the coffin, staining the glass with my tears. Giorgio wept in the cattle shed, and the cattle wept with him. Sandro and Mario wept over their game of chess, and Antonio says he could hear nothing over the radio but the sound of distant weeping. Only Gian Petro did not weep but his eyes were tense and bewildered, full of fear in a way I had never seen before. He brought me the glass, from where I do not know, and he told me my craft would be tested as never before. In spite of my grief, I was proud when we laid her in the coffin of glass. Every detail was perfect, the glass cut and fitted and sealed so there was no sign of joining, no hint of workmanship, no evidence of the craft that was behind the art. The coffin was as perfect as any jewel, as impervious to the elements as any rock.

Someone is responsible, and I fear it may be me. We were warned never to leave her alone, even for a second, and she was warned never to open the door to any knock. I had gone to the cattle shed for a moment to speak with Giorgio. Sandro and Mario left their game of chess for a moment to bring her an icicle from the roof because she had teased them into getting it for her. She loved to suck on icicles like a child with a frozen treat. Antonio was at his listening post and Guido was fishing in his frozen stream. Gian Petro was in the village, as usual. There was a knock, there must have been a knock, she opened the door, she must have opened it herself against all the warnings, and when I returned she was dead, a piece of apple lodged in her throat. The rest of the apple sat on the table, its skin as red as blood, its flesh as white as milk.

Gian Petro was in a rage when he returned a few moments later. I could tell him nothing, only confess my lack of responsibility, my failure. Sandro and Mario, from their position on the roof, saw a flapping of black rags in the street, like a giant crow, but thought it was only one of the crones of the village passing. A sudden cold wind nearly blew them from the roof and they had to cling to the chimney until it passed.

Then, that terrible night, the coldest night of the year, we carried her in her coffin up into the mountain. Gian Petro broke the trail through the deep snow, and we six struggled behind him, stumbling on our tiny legs, though the coffin with its treasure inside weighed no more than a tiny bird. It was both the lightest and the heaviest load I have ever had to bear.

And now what are we to do? There is no longer any point to the making of sabots or the catching of eels, no point to the raising of cattle or the making of wine, no point to the working of metal or to listening to the reports of a war about which I no longer care. My heart tells me that this war will never end, that spring will never come again. We shall only have war and winter, winter and war.

Mario

This place is full of fear and pain. In the darkness of this dungeon we replay a medieval battle of light against darkness, good against evil. Throughout history, this castle has been the head of the valley, the centre from which wisdom and morality spread to the sprawling body of the community, but now there is a cancer working here, a foreign body that has seized control and whose evil seeps outward, infecting the whole.

The villagers led the Nazis to our door, and who can blame them, full of fear and superstition, trying to save themselves at any cost. They have allied themselves with a failing demon, though they cannot know that. They clustered around the soldiers who dragged us from our beds, they jeered and shouted and their faces were filled with hate, our weakness as hateful to them as the Nazis' strength.

The war will be over in a few days, but that will be too late for us. We are in the coils of a dying but still-dangerous monster. At dawn the firing squad, they have told us, after our week of pain. And so our mission fails, or else we have done our part in some larger plan that has no further use for us. The girl was innocence itself, she loved and mothered us, and her death, I think, is the death of innocence and goodness in this world. Perhaps the Nazis will be replaced with some even larger evil, though it is hard to think what evil might be greater.

We have been tortured and mutilated beyond anything I thought the human body could bear. And they used the tools of my trade, the metal-worker's tools, pincers and tongs and fire. They have slowly removed our fingernails, crushed our arms and legs, set fire to our hair and carved their hateful symbol in our flesh with a burning poker. We have told them nothing, though there is nothing to tell but the location of a mountain grave, a glass coffin and a body they might defile but could not offer pain. Tomorrow they will ask us one more time, then they will pour the hot lead of bullets into our bodies, whatever our answer.

I am almost eager for that death. See us for what we were, what we are. Our bodies stunted and deformed, half men always on the lookout for the kick, the beating that the others must give because we affront them by wrapping desire in such awkward flesh. We are comic at a distance, terrifying when we're near, conjuring in every man the dwarf within.

And though I am eager, I am sick with loss. I yearn for one more taste of the water from a cool stream, for the scent of roses on a heavy summer day, for the scratch of wool on my skin. I want to see clouds low over the mountains, to hear Guido sing a song full of joy. I ache for the world that will end in the morning.

Here in this tiny dark cell we seven are huddled as if we were one flesh. We cannot tell whose moan we hear, even when it is our own. The warm blood we feel is ours communally, the fear we share, one common fear. Only Gian Petro has hope and his soft voice is murmuring words of comfort, but it is too late. Hope is the final torture, the last delusion. We have given our lives to a mission that is probably a failure, may even have been a chimera from the start.

Now, the first rays of dawn will be spreading from the east. The soldiers will be oiling their guns and preparing the blindfolds. There will be one large grave waiting in the courtyard, a bag of quicklime beside it. They will be so intent on their task that perhaps they will not hear the soft thunder of the bombs that rock even our cell below the castle, the distant rumbling of the guns.

Gian Petro

This is a spring that takes itself seriously, that believes in the history of transformation and is not satisfied with the simple mechanics of budding and flowering. When the bomb landed on the castle, opening the cocoon of our cell, I stepped across the broken bricks of the wall into a blazing dawn. The clouds had curled themselves into balls of cumulus and were dreaming along the horizon to the south. I looked for the others, Giorgio, Sandro, Antonio, Guido, Rico, Mario, but they had disappeared. I reached my long arms into the air, stretched my long legs, felt the strength ripple through my body. Then I heard the voices inside me. Little Guido, whispering to me, told me where to look for old Snapper, the dark one. Giorgio told me where the cattle liked to feed, Rico sent a message to my fingers telling me the exact pressure of a chisel on wood, Mario sent a vision of a bracelet wound from gold chains and Antonio let me hear the whistle of crickets in a distant stream.

And then I knew that the first miracle had occurred. In the crucible of that exploding bomb, our mass of deformed dwarf-flesh had separated into atoms, then reformed into molecules. The molecules had re-knit themselves into amino acids and proteins, shaped themselves into complex chains, twisted and curled into the only possible body. The accidental electricity of that explosion had charged that body with life and filled each neuron and synapse of the brain with seven memories. It had concentrated all the ghosts of the castle, all thoughts that had been thought there, all the passions that had seeped into the stone walls of the castle and delivered them to us, to me. I realized that I had been born that second, and so I named myself. Gian Petro.

When Gian Petro stepped into the courtyard, out of the ruins of the castle, he saw that thousands of mushrooms had sprung up during the night. They formed a soft bed, like velvet, and as he strode across them, crushing them, they exuded a delicate milky substance that smelled, not unpleasantly, like bleach. Beyond the gates of the castle, the open field that led to the village was filled with snow-white flowers, each with a core of crimson. Along the wall that separated field from road, the vines were covered with mauve trumpet flowers that whispered to him softly. There were bees everywhere, humming ecstatically.

The village was full of music. People were singing and dancing in the streets. An old man played a violin, dancing as he played, and a young man accompanied him on an accordion. The villagers had shed their winter black and were dressed in bright reds and yellows and blues. A pretty girl swirled by, her red dress so bright it seemed in flames. Her lover wore a white shirt, open at the neck, with a brilliant red bandana. "Baron," they called to Gian Petro, "the war is over. The war is over." He smiled at his people's joy, but he kept walking through the village, past the tables heaped with food and wine, past the donkeys with garlands around their necks, down the winding path into the valley.

The grass was so lush along the pathway that sometimes it was hard to tell where it wound. The vineyards along the slope were a riot of leaves and the grapes, though not yet ripe, seemed ready to burst with sweetness. Underground, the roots were burying themselves deep, searching for water. They passed underground messages up through the sap to the highest leaves of the trees. Brilliant birds flashed yellow and red in the blur of green.

The baron continued onward, down through the valley into the forest. Under the pine and spruce, it was cool, and sunlight dappled the carpet of needles. He came to a small, fast-running stream, and followed it to a pool deep in the heart of the forest. There, the body of the drowned soldier had surfaced. It was surrounded by a mass of white water lilies, and water lilies seemed to be growing out of the flesh. Gian Petro pulled the body from the pool and laid it gently on the grassy shore. Then he drew a line and hook from his pocket and baited the hook with the white root of a small willow. He tossed out his line into the pool, and the dark one rose to the bait. Gian Petro pulled him in without effort and laid him on the bank beside the dead soldier. They were exactly the same size, and from a small distance, it was impossible to tell them apart.

Gian Petro followed the stream a little further, till it turned, then he continued up the mountain on the other side of the valley. The trees soon became sparser and were replaced with gentian and saxifrage and rock jasmine. When he reached the very top of the mountain where the glass coffin lay, he saw that it was surrounded by snowdrops and tiny red bloodflowers. He strode across the carpet of flowers, not caring how the sap bled from the tiny plants he crushed. He opened the lid of the glass coffin, picked up the girl and laid her down in the flowers. The piece of apple that had stuck in her throat came free, and she breathed. Her pale white cheeks turned red with life as he took her in his arms. He spoke to her of love in his seven voices, and as they loved, the discreet sun hid his face behind a cloud. Every living thing reached up eagerly to the gentle rain that followed.